# ANIMALS of —— FARTHING WOOD

## The Story Continues . . .

# The
# ANIMALS
## —— of ——
# FARTHING
# WOOD

## The Story Continues . . .

### COLIN DANN

Red Fox

A Red Fox Book

Published by Random House Children's Books
20 Vauxhall Bridge Road, London SW1V 2SA

A division of Random House UK Ltd
London Melbourne Sydney Auckland
Johannesburg and agencies throughout the world

First published by Red Fox 1994

3 5 7 9 10 8 6 4

Set in Bembo by SX Composing Ltd, Rayleigh, Essex
Printed and bound in Great Britain by
Cox & Wyman Ltd, Reading, Berkshire

Random House UK Limited Reg. No. 954009

ISBN 0 09 937441 2

# CONTENTS

# Part 1

# IN THE GRIP OF WINTER

# CHAPTER ONE

The animals of Farthing Wood were facing their first winter in their new home in the Nature Reserve of White Deer Park. They had travelled there together after they had to leave Farthing Wood because it was being destroyed by humans.

As the winter days grew shorter and colder Adder and Toad knew they must find a spot for hibernation. They chose a hole in a bank where the earth was soft.

'This is ideal,' said Adder, beginning to enter the hole.

'Wait!' cried Toad. 'Aren't you going to say goodbye to the other animals before you hibernate?'

'Goodbye? Nonsense,' the snake hissed. 'No-one seeks me out when I'm around, so they will hardly miss me when I'm not.' She wriggled into the bank.

Toad shrugged. Adder had never been known for the warmth of her feelings. 'I'll join you later,' he called after her.

Toad shivered as he set off to find his friends. A cold wind was blowing across the Park.

Badger was out looking for food. He saw Toad coming towards him and greeted him, 'Toad, my dear friend! Isn't it a little chilly for you?'

'A bit,' said Toad. 'But I just wanted to say good-bye and good luck before I hibernate.'

'How kind,' said Badger. 'And we'll all need luck, Toad. I can sense the winter is going to be a hard one.'

'Yes. I don't envy you and Fox and the others,' said Toad. 'I am lucky. I can just go to sleep and only wake up when it's warmer again.'

Fox and Tawny Owl joined them.

'Go deep underground, Toad,' Fox advised the little creature. 'There is going to be some very cold weather.'

Toad nodded. 'See you in the spring,' he said.

As October passed into November the leaves fell thickly. Squirrels, voles and fieldmice feasted on the crop of autumn fruit and berries. There were plenty of worms and slugs, and Mole and Badger made short work of them.

One day the first snow fell. Mole, whose tunnels connected with Badger's sett, was visiting his old friend. The two peered out at the wintry scene. Mole had never seen snow before. 'Will it cover everything?' he asked Badger.

'Oh no,' Badger replied. 'But many small birds and animals will find it difficult to find food. In severe weather many of them could die.'

Mole looked solemn. 'I–I'm glad we can dig, Badger,' he said. 'Away from the snow.'

Some days later the animals saw the Warden of the

4

Nature Reserve on his rounds. Here and there he stopped to tie something on to a low branch. When the man was out of sight Fox and Badger went to investigate.

'It's food,' said Badger. 'For the birds.'

'Then it's a sure sign he expects things to be really bad,' Fox said grimly. He looked at Badger. 'I'm worried,' he admitted. 'If this snow continues, we're all of us going to be in difficulties.'

'We'll manage,' Badger said. 'What else is the Oath for if not to help each other at times like these?'

## CHAPTER TWO

As the year drew to a close, a fiercely cold frost held the Park in its grip night after night. The ground was as hard as iron and thick ice formed on the Park's pond. Even the stream that ran through the Park was frozen along its edges. Whistler the heron and his mate found it hard to get fish from the stream.

'We shall have to fish further upstream,' said the female heron. 'The water runs more swiftly there and we can catch crayfish.'

'Whatever you say,' Whistler answered. 'You know the area best.'

His mate's idea was a good one. The herons caught several crayfish each and also a few fish. They had soon eaten their fill.

'We mustn't be selfish,' Whistler said. He knew times were hard for his friends. 'This food could be good for others too. I'm going to look for Fox and see if I can be of any use.'

Fox was away from his den but Vixen was sitting at the entrance. Whistler was surprised to see how thin she looked.

'Food is so scarce,' Vixen told the heron. 'Fox has

gone to find out for himself how the others are coping.'

'I think I can help,' said Whistler. He told Vixen about the crayfish. 'I'd be delighted to catch some for you.'

Vixen drooled at the thought of food. 'We'd be so grateful,' she said. 'Shall we wait for Fox?'

'Certainly.'

After a while, Whistler saw the familiar figure of Fox on his way back home across the gleaming white snow. Weasel was with Fox. The friends welcomed each other. Then Fox became serious. 'Things are even worse than I expected,' he said to Vixen. 'The voles and fieldmice can't survive this cold – they're dying. And some of the older rabbits have perished too.'

Whistler knew that this was bad news. But he was even more alarmed by Fox's appearance. Gone was the strong and healthy beast who had led the Farthing Wood party across the countryside to their new home. In his place was a weak and starving creature. The much smaller Weasel looked in far better shape.

Vixen tried to cheer her partner by the news of Whistler's offer.

'It'd be something good to eat at last,' she said, 'rather than worms and slugs and carrion.'

'Good for us, yes,' Fox admitted. 'But not much use to voles or fieldmice.' He seemed to have the cares of the entire community on his shoulders.

'You must keep up your strength,' Vixen urged him. 'You'll be in a better state to help them then.'

7

Whistler led the three animals away. As they went they discussed their other friends. Tawny Owl and Kestrel were managing reasonably well, as were Hare and his family, while the squirrels had tucked themselves up in their dreys during the bitter weather.

'Did you see Badger?' Whistler asked.

'No. Strange to say, although it's daylight, he wasn't at home,' Fox replied. 'But I've no worries on his account. He's been through bad winters before.'

Whistler lost no time in spearing some food for the hungry foxes and Weasel. He was well rewarded by their hearty thanks. Full stomachs made for lighter hearts as they returned home in the dusk. But their more cheerful mood ended abruptly. Mole was waiting for them at the foxes' earth. He was very agitated.

'What's wrong?' Fox asked at once.

'Badger's disappeared,' Mole answered, beginning to sob.

'Calm down, Mole,' Fox tried to soothe him. 'That's nothing unusual, is it? He's always out looking for food at dusk.'

'No, no.' Mole shook his head. 'You don't understand. He's been missing all day as well. He *never* goes far in the daytime.'

Fox nodded. 'That's true. I missed him earlier. When did you last see him?'

'Yesterday,' said Mole. 'We were talking about the awful weather and – and – the lack of food and

8

Badger said he was concerned about you, Fox, because it wasn't fair for you alone to feel responsible for everyone else. And – and – he thought you needed some help.'

'Dear kind Badger,' Vixen said softly.

'Oh yes, now I see,' said Fox. 'He's gone off on some venture of his own; goodness knows what he thinks he can do, though. Don't worry, Mole. He'll be back soon. I'll ask Tawny Owl to keep a look-out for him.'

But Badger didn't return, and there was no sign of him. The next morning Fox set out on a search. The powdery snow that blanketed the Park was tiring to walk on and Fox's feet sank into it at every step. He knew he would never be able to cover the entire Reserve. He skirted the Hollow – the animals' meeting-place – and went round the area where the Farthing Wood band had settled. Pretty soon Fox was panting with the effort.

'Badger could be anywhere. I need help,' he muttered to himself. 'Kestrel has the most piercing eyesight – she can scan the whole Park from the air.'

Then Fox saw a group of white deer ahead, amongst them the Great Stag. The deer were feeding from bales of hay provided by the Park Warden. The Stag stepped forward.

'How are you and your friends managing?' he asked Fox.

'We're coping as best we can,' he replied. 'But it's not easy.'

'Luckily we have human help,' the Stag said. 'But I'm afraid grass is no use to a fox.'

'No, it isn't. However, if you could spare a few stalks for the mice and rabbits, that would be a great help.'

'Hm. I don't see why not,' the Stag said. 'This touching concern of yours for other creatures, Fox, is very unusual.'

'We Farthing Wood animals try to help one another,' Fox explained simply. 'Perhaps you could drop a few mouthfuls of hay by the Hollow?'

'I shall see to it,' the Stag nodded. 'And what are you doing out in daylight?'

'I'm searching for Badger,' Fox replied. 'He's gone missing. I don't suppose you have come across him?'

The White Stag shook his head. 'No, but if I do, I'll let you know. It really is most unusual how you animals care for one another.'

Fox continued on, his aim to locate Kestrel. It began to snow again. Fox kept going and at last, close to the Warden's cottage, he found Kestrel perched on a fence-post. The bird swooped down to greet him. Fox explained his errand.

'I've seen neither hide nor hair of Badger,' Kestrel remarked. 'But don't worry, I'll go at once to look. If he's anywhere in the Park, I'll spot him.'

But as Kestrel took to the air, Fox began to wonder what they would do if Badger weren't found.

By the time he had got back to the Hollow, Fox was worn out. Vixen, Tawny Owl, Weasel, Mole and Hare were waiting there, shifting their feet in the biting cold. It was still snowing.

'Is there – any news?' Mole asked tearfully.

'Not yet, but Kestrel's bound to find him,' Fox replied with more confidence than he actually felt.

Eventually the bird returned. 'I'm sorry,' she said. 'I've had no luck at all.'

Mole sobbed aloud. Vixen tried to comfort him.

'I can't understand it,' Kestrel said. 'I've flown over the reserve twice. Badger seems to have disappeared into thin air.'

'He can't just have vanished,' said Fox. 'There's something strange about this.'

'He must have been captured,' Weasel suggested.

'By what? There's no animal large enough to do it,' Fox argued.

'Well, there's nothing we can do for the moment,' Tawny Owl said. 'We can't stand around in this weather. I have to catch my supper. And that's not easy these days.' She flew off and the other animals began to scatter. As they did, a number of white deer, led by the Great Stag, approached the Hollow carrying mouthfuls of hay. They dropped these in a pile.

'Hare, will you tell the rabbits about this?' Fox asked him.

Hare was already nibbling at a grass–stem. He nodded silently.

'And Weasel, could you alert the voles and mice? I'm simply too tired to go myself.'

'Of course,' Weasel replied. 'You go and rest.'

11

Mole trailed behind the others. 'Badger *can't* have disappeared,' he whispered to himself. 'I'll find him. Somehow.'

The missing Badger had left home with the best of intentions. His idea was to find some of the creatures who had always lived in White Deer Park. He thought their greater knowledge of the Park might be of use to his friends who had such problems getting enough to eat. But, apart from a stoat who looked as famished as the Farthing Wood animals, Badger didn't manage to speak to anyone.

He was heading down an icy slope when suddenly his feet slid from under him. He skidded helplessly down to the bottom and crashed against a rock.

'Oh no,' Badger groaned in great pain. He tried to get up but one of his legs was injured and he collapsed again in agony.

He lay there in the stinging cold for a whole night. In the morning he was so numb and stiff he could barely move at all, and certainly couldn't stand.

Fortunately, help was at hand. The Warden, who had been out dumping hay for the deer, was surveying the Park through his field-glasses. He picked out Badger's body and went to investigate. The helpless creature was examined and Badger found himself being lifted and carried away. The next time he opened his eyes he was in the warmth and comfort of the Warden's cottage kitchen.

Badger was put into a dog basket which had been carefully lined with sacking. He didn't complain. He sensed the man meant to help him. The Warden prepared some food – warm milk and raw mince – and placed it in front of the basket. Badger was able to reach it without much effort.

The man was delighted with the animal's appetite, but he didn't stay. Badger was left alone to eat and rest. 'Oh dear,' said Badger to himself, 'a lot of good I was to my friends. Now they won't know where I am and I won't know what's happening to them.' He sank back and, since he was very weak, he was soon asleep.

When he woke again it was evening. A fresh supply of food had been left. The room was dark but for the moonlight shining in. An animal voice spoke close at hand.

'You're in a bad way.'

Badger twisted his head. A cat was coolly padding towards him. It paused and sniffed at him. It was a ginger cat.

'You smell of the wild,' it announced. Then the cat said, 'Have you been eating my meat?'

'The man fed me,' Badger managed to mutter.

'There's no problem,' the cat answered. 'There's plenty more where that came from. What do you usually eat?'

'Worms, grubs, roots, small creatures . . .' Badger replied.

'Rats?'

'Sometimes.'

'Really?' The cat seemed interested. 'We have something in common. I hunt rats myself.'

13

'Are there many hereabouts?' Badger asked eagerly, thinking of Owl and the foxes.

'Not since I arrived,' the cat answered smugly, flexing its claws.

Just then the Warden returned. Instantly the cat began purring and rubbing itself affectionately against the man's legs. The Warden spoke to his cat and began to prepare him a meal. He spoke to Badger too and Badger easily sensed the man's kindness.

After the cat's meal was over, he and the Warden left Badger alone. The cat turned at the door and said, 'I hope you're comfortable for now? We'll talk again later.'

Badger looked forward to this. He thought the ginger cat a very interesting character who could give him advice. Outside, the snow was falling again. Badger thought of the hardship his friends were facing every moment and felt guilty at his own cosiness. How he wished they could all share it.

## CHAPTER THREE

The next day, well rested and fed, Badger felt a little better. However, his leg was still painful. The ginger cat came into the kitchen with snowflakes melting on his fur.

'Brrr.' He shivered. 'You're well out of that,' he told Badger. 'It's freezing. You owe the man a lot.'

'I know,' said Badger. 'But make no mistake, Cat, we wild creatures can look after ourselves. If I hadn't been injured . . .'

'But you were,' the cat purred sweetly. He went to lap at a bowl of milk. Then he turned to Badger. 'Tell me about your life. I'd like to hear your story,' he said.

Badger was only too willing. He told the cat about his underground home, his friends, and about how they had all made the journey from far away in Farthing Wood. The cat was very impressed.

'So you took the mice along as food, did you?' he asked.

'No, no, not at all,' Badger corrected him. 'The voles and fieldmice were our companions. Before we set out we all promised to protect each others' safety.'

15

'An unusual collection of animals,' the cat commented.

Human voices were heard outside. The cat glanced up. 'Oh, here comes the man who makes animals well,' he told Badger. 'He often comes here to tend wild creatures.'

Sure enough the vet had come to examine Badger. Badger felt no fear. His leg was dressed and securely bandaged. The vet gave his head a friendly stroke and he and the Warden left again. Badger fell to thinking once more about his friends. Every so often he looked across at the ginger cat who was dozing on the window-sill. Badger was trying to come to a decision.

At last he said, 'I'd like you to do me a favour if you would.'

The cat half opened his eyes.

'I'm so very worried about my friends in the Park,' Badger went on. 'I know they'll be searching for me and, really, things are so tough for them just now, simply trying to survive, I don't want them bothering about me.'

'I think I know what's coming,' the cat remarked.

'Would you be able to carry a message to them?' Badger blurted out. 'You'd be in no danger. Fox and Vixen sleep in the daytime so there would be no risk.'

'I'm not afraid of foxes,' the cat replied airily. 'But how would I know where to go? White Deer Park is so big. And the conditions out there are awful. It would be too long a trek there and back.'

Badger sighed. 'Then I've no choice,' he said. 'I must go myself.'

'Don't be so silly,' hissed the cat. 'How could *you* go? Oh very well, if I must,' he grumbled. 'You'd better give me directions.'

Badger was delighted. 'I'll never forget this,' he said. 'And neither will my friends. I'm so grateful. Now, here's how to find them . . .'

The cat listened carefully.

Next day the weather was clear. The frost overnight had frozen the ground solid. Ginger Cat emerged from the cottage. He tested the snow with a front paw. It felt quite firm. He began his journey.

Meanwhile, from another part of the Park, Mole was continuing his search. But Mole was using a different method. He was searching underground, because he had thought that if Badger was not to be found on the surface, perhaps he was lost underground. He scoured every tunnel he knew and some he didn't, and then dug some new ones. Every so often he poked his head out in the daylight to see where he was. Then he continued.

So Ginger Cat and Mole approached each other by their different routes. Mole suddenly saw a large unfamiliar animal coming towards him. He ducked back underground.

'Wait!' called Ginger Cat. Mole was the first creature he had seen and he wanted help. 'I'm looking for Badger's friends. Are you – '

Mole's head popped out at once. 'Badger? Is he alive? Where is he?'

17

Ginger Cat explained. 'He's quite well. He was injured but the man is caring for him.'

'The man?'

'Your Warden.'

'Oh, what wonderful news,' Mole exclaimed. 'I'm so relieved. How kind of you to come. When will Badger return?'

'That I can't say,' Ginger Cat replied. 'You'll pass the message on, won't you?'

'Oh yes,' Mole said. 'At once. And please, tell Badger we're all right too. And – and – we miss him.'

The cat turned, only too happy to be done with his task and to get back to warmth and shelter. Mole watched him and then ran a little way after him. 'Won't you come and meet the others?' he called.

Ginger Cat was too far ahead to hear what Mole had said. He trotted back. 'What?'

At that moment Kestrel, who was still scanning the Park for signs of Badger, was hovering above. She saw Ginger Cat rush towards Mole and mistook the action for an attack. Instantly she dived to the rescue, plummeting downwards and digging her talons into Ginger Cat's back.

The cat howled and lashed out at the bird, but Kestrel was already winging upward again.

'No! No!' Mole cried. 'Stop, Kestrel! He's a friend!'

Kestrel prepared for another swoop. Mole tried to shield Ginger Cat, and Kestrel hesitated.

'He's friendly,' Mole shrilled. 'He's brought news of Badger.'

Kestrel landed and apologized for her mistake. 'It looked to me as though you were being pounced on,' she explained.

'You and your wretched Oath!' Ginger Cat miaowed angrily. 'You've wounded me.' Blood was flowing from his back.

'Oh dear,' said Mole. 'You'll need some help. Kestrel, you'd better fetch Fox. The poor cat's badly injured.'

Fox came quickly and was most upset. 'What a way to reward your kindness,' he said. 'Come and rest in our den, Cat. We'll clean your wounds for you.'

Ginger Cat allowed himself to be led away.

Inside the foxes' earth Vixen licked gently at Ginger Cat's fur. The wounded animal relaxed under the foxes' care and presently fell asleep.

'He'll need feeding,' said Fox. 'We must go hunting for him, Vixen.'

At dusk the foxes set off, leaving Mole to keep Ginger Cat company. While they were gone the cat awoke.

'How do you feel?' Mole asked with concern.

'Much better for that nap,' Ginger Cat replied. 'No need for me to stay any longer. I must get back.'

Mole tried to get him to stay.

'Nonsense. I'll be all right,' the cat insisted. 'I'm glad to have met you and Fox and Vixen.' He pulled himself out through the entrance hole. 'Farewell, Mole.' He padded off towards the cottage. 'But as for that Kestrel,' he vowed to himself, 'if I ever get the chance, I'll get even with her.'

## CHAPTER FOUR

Ginger Cat was exhausted when he reached home. He limped through his cat-flap and fell asleep on the carpet. It was night. In the morning the Warden had to attend to his pet's scratches and then, at last, Badger had a chance to ask the cat what had happened.

'Did you manage to pass on my message?' Badger asked eagerly.

'Oh yes. I met Mole and Fox and Vixen. They were all relieved to hear your news. And *this*' – Ginger Cat showed his wounds – 'was how Kestrel greeted me!'

Badger was shocked. 'But – but – ' he spluttered. Ginger Cat described Kestrel's attack. 'Oh, how awful,' Badger cried feelingly. 'And you were doing me a kindness. But I can see how it happened – a tragic accident. I'm sure Kestrel must be very sorry.'

Ginger Cat didn't comment on that. But he said, 'I know one thing. I wouldn't like your kind of life. I've seen an underground home now and how you live. Give me warmth, shelter and regular food every time. You can keep your so-called freedom. You should see what it's done for your fox friends.

20

They're so skinny you wouldn't see them if they turned sideways.'

Badger gulped. He hated to hear this news and he felt more guilty than ever.

The days passed and Badger's leg healed. He practised walking around and one evening the Warden decided he was fit enough to be released. Badger's bandages had been removed long ago and, because of the good food and care he had received, he looked sleeker and plumper than he had done for a long time.

An icy blast met him as he stepped outside the cosy cottage. Badger hesitated, then the Warden gave him a gentle shove. He was on his own now! He trotted forward and turned for a last look at his recent comfortable home. Ginger Cat was framed in the doorway.

'Farewell for now,' said Badger. 'Thank you for your company. I know we shall meet again.'

'Until then,' Ginger Cat replied.

Badger soon reached his sett. It seemed unfamiliar and cheerless. Mole, who had been looking in hopefully every day, was waiting for him. But when he saw Badger, who now looked so different, he held back.

'It's all right, Mole. It *is* me,' said Badger.

'Oh Badger, we've all missed you so,' said Mole. 'It's marvellous to have you back. But you look – '

'Fatter?' Badger finished for him. 'Probably am, Mole. I've been very well fed. Can't think how I'm going to adjust to my old life, but perhaps I won't have to.'

Mole was puzzled. Badger's manner didn't seem quite the same.

'I'm going to see Fox and Vixen,' Badger told him.

Tawny Owl spied Badger as he trotted to the foxes' earth. She flew down. 'Welcome back. My, you have grown plump.'

Badger scowled but said nothing.

Fox and Vixen were out hunting so Badger waited for their return. Presently they arrived back. They slunk into their earth, weary and weak. It was a while before they had strength enough to speak. Badger was terribly alarmed by the way they looked.

At last Fox said, 'It's good to have you back with us, Badger.' Then, eyeing Badger's sleek appearance, he added shrewdly, 'You will be staying now?'

'With you, yes,' Badger answered promptly. 'But why here? I've got a wonderful idea.'

'Whatever is it?' Vixen asked.

'I can see what a hard time you've had,' Badger said. 'And you can't go on like this. There's only one solution. You must all come back with me to the Warden's cottage and put yourselves in his care.'

'What on earth are you talking about?' Fox demanded. 'We're wild creatures. We have to survive on our own.'

'But you're not, are you? Why, look at you!' cried Badger. 'No, Fox, it's your only hope. Believe me.'

'You're being absurd,' Fox grunted. 'How could the Warden help us?'

'He helped *me*,' Badger replied.

'You were injured,' Vixen pointed out. 'We're not.'

'But look how you're suffering. The man is concerned for all of us. He'll *have* to feed you.'

'Your spell in human care has turned your head,' Fox remarked. 'How could the entire population of White Deer Park get into the man's cottage?'

'I'm trying to help the Farthing Wood animals,' said Badger. 'But I can't force you.' He was angry that Fox didn't agree with him. 'If you want to die of starvation, that's up to you. But don't expect me to join you.'

The foxes were so stunned by the change in Badger that they watched him leave their earth without a word.

Tawny Owl had been listening outside the den. 'Going back to your friend the cat?' she asked Badger icily.

'Yes, I am,' Badger snapped. He was fuming. 'It seems he's my only friend now.'

When Fox and Vixen had recovered a little, Vixen said, 'Whatever can we do?'

'Nothing,' Fox answered bluntly. 'Badger must find out for himself how foolish he's being.'

And in due course Badger did. He trudged slowly across the Park, intent on returning to the comfort of the cottage. In the early morning light he found Ginger Cat sitting outside his master's dwelling.

23

Badger greeted him joyfully. 'Hallo. It's me – Badger. I'm back.'

'So I see,' the cat answered coolly.

'Aren't you pleased to see me?' Badger asked with disappointment.

'I'm astonished to see you at all.'

'But I've come back. For good,' Badger explained.

The cat yawned. 'I think you're in for a surprise,' he said. 'Your stay with us is over. You're fit and well again.'

'We'll see about that,' Badger growled.

Just then the door opened. The Warden came out and gave a little cry of pleasure at Badger's appearance. Badger felt encouraged and tried to enter the cottage but the man chuckled and firmly pushed him away, closing the door again and leaving Badger on the outside.

'You see?' drawled the cat.

Badger did see. It was as though he had awakened from a dream. How could he ever have been so stupid? He wasn't a pet like Ginger Cat, but an animal from the Wild, who belonged in the outside world. How could he have thought otherwise? He had made himself look very silly. He blundered through the snow, eager to get away.

Kestrel, who missed nothing that moved over the ground, had witnessed it all. When she saw Badger pushed away, and then his hurried exit from the cottage, she dived down and joined him on the ground. 'You're going the right way this time, Badger,' she cried gladly.

'Yes, Kestrel,' Badger muttered. 'What a stupid creature I've been.'

Behind them Ginger Cat was watching everything. Now he saw his chance for revenge. He crept stealthily forward on his noiseless feet. Then he put on a spurt and leapt on the unsuspecting bird, clawing and biting at his victim. Kestrel screeched and battled to free herself.

Badger was horrified. For a moment he wasn't sure what to do. The cat had been his friend and had done him a good turn. But it didn't take him long to remember where his true loyalties lay. The Oath!

Badger rushed to the bird's defence, bringing all his weight and strength to bear on the cat. He got a grip on Ginger Cat's neck. Kestrel got free and flew away. Now the fight was between the two animals on the ground. The cat howled and spat and clawed but Badger's greater strength began to tell. He knew he had the cat at his mercy and he could have killed him. But now he had to repay his debt. He stepped away, panting heavily. Ginger Cat sped like an arrow back to safety.

Kestrel screeched from the air, 'A thousand thanks, Badger. Welcome back.'

'All clear now,' Badger called. 'Come down and let me see to your hurts.'

Kestrel was quickly beside him. Badger licked at the scratches. 'These will soon heal,' he said. 'From now on, I'm a Farthing Wood animal again. We all live or die together.'

## CHAPTER FIVE

Kestrel flew to tell Fox and Vixen the good news. 'Badger saved my life,' she announced.

'That makes me very happy,' said Fox. 'Now we should all meet together to welcome him back. Let's gather in Badger's sett.'

Badger was feeling rather nervous as he approached his home. He wasn't sure of his friends' reception after he had been so foolish. He found Whistler outside who immediately reassured him.

'Don't worry,' said the heron. 'You're a hero again. Kestrel has told everyone how you saved her.'

Badger took a deep breath and entered his sett. The animals greeted him enthusiastically. To many who hadn't seen him for weeks, like Weasel, Hare, the rabbits, squirrels and mice, he was just a long-lost friend. Tawny Owl, the foxes and Mole were simply delighted to have the real Badger back. No-one mentioned his recent strangeness.

Badger was saddened to see how the numbers of the smaller animals had dwindled. He cleared his throat. 'Friends,' he began, 'my spell in human care has taught me an important lesson. Man is an important source of food.' He looked around, then went on hastily in case the others were wondering if he was going to talk more nonsense. 'We can tap that source of food.'

'Not the Warden again,' Weasel groaned.

'No, no,' Badger shook his head. 'My idea is to make use of human help without their knowing it.'

'How can we do that?' Rabbit asked.

'Well, we all know humans waste almost as much food as they eat. Now, *we* would find that waste very useful.'

'You mean, scavenge?' Tawny Owl asked loftily.

'Why not?' Badger replied. 'It could mean the difference between life and death for some of you.'

'It's an excellent idea,' said Fox. 'Go on, Badger.'

Badger warmed to his theme. 'If you remember, Toad told us about some houses in an area outside the Park. It was from one of those that he began his journey home to Farthing Wood. Now, each one of those houses has people who waste food. We only have to find where they dump it.'

'That's simple,' said Kestrel. 'I know – I've seen them doing it.'

'Good,' said Badger. 'So it needs the fittest of us – that's me at present – to go and fetch it. And the birds can go with me. They'll easily be able to carry supplies back of anything useful.'

'I'll go with you,' Fox decided. 'I know I'm not as fit as I have been, but just try and leave me out.'

So, that very night, with Tawny Owl leading the

way, Badger, Fox, Kestrel and Whistler headed for the Park boundary. Owl flew on ahead to find their route. They found her waiting for them.

'We shall have to be cautious,' she told them. 'There are others around on the same errand.'

'Foxes?'

'Yes, two of them,' Owl answered.

'Hm. Well, we shouldn't be surprised,' Fox commented. 'We're not the only ones desperate for food.'

Fox and Badger scrambled under the fence where animals had previously scraped away the soil. They crossed a ditch and went along a road where there was a row of houses.

'Wait here,' said Tawny Owl by the first of these. 'I'll scout ahead.'

She had no luck with the first house, nor the second. These had walls and gates too high for the animals to get over. The next house was some distance away from the others and had a large garden. Inside the garden two young foxes were nosing around some sheds and hutches. Owl heard some nervous clucks from inside them. She flew back quickly.

'There are chickens in there and the foxes are after them,' she reported excitedly.

Fox's ears pricked up. 'Chickens, eh?'

'There might be enough for all of us,' Badger suggested, 'if we're quick.'

They ran to the fence surrounding the garden. It was low. The three birds fluttered into the garden.

'I'm no jumper,' said Badger. 'Can you manage the fence, Fox?'

'Easily, if I were properly fit,' Fox answered. 'But now – well, I don't know. I'll have a jolly good try though.' He backed away to give himself a good run-up. Badger watched him leap, just skimming the fence-top, but landing safely. There was no way in for Badger who could only skulk by the fence.

Suddenly he heard a loud crash, followed by the sound of clattering wings and frenzied squawks. A dog began to bark furiously and then there were human shouts. Before Badger quite knew what to do, two foxes leapt over the fence into the road. Each one carried a hen in its jaws. They raced away as fast as they could. There were three of four gun-shots. Badger cowered down just as a third fox – his own friend – leapt the fence almost on top of him.

'Quickly!' cried Fox. 'This way!' He pelted away in the opposite direction from that taken by the other two foxes. Badger loped after him and just got clear of the house before a huge and ferocious dog bounded out of a gate followed by two men with shotguns. The dog galloped after the chicken thieves. Fox and Badger dived under a parked car. Human voices shouted, calling back the furious dog. Then two more shots rang out. The pair of young foxes dropped like stones, as dead as the slaughtered chickens.

Fox and Badger watched the men examine the fox carcasses, then hurl them into the ditch on the other side of the road while the dog frisked around them.

Each man picked up a hen, then they trudged back to the house.

A little later Tawny Owl came swooping over the fence. She found Fox and Badger safe. 'Thank heavens you're still alive,' she said.

'Alive but still without food,' Badger remarked.

'There are hens all over the place,' said Owl. 'Those young foxes overturned the coop and they're running around frantically.'

'No use to us,' Fox grunted. 'I couldn't go back in there.'

'I'm going to look around farther down this road,' Badger announced. 'We simply can't go back without something.' He trotted away while Owl went to look in the garden again.

Fox stayed where he was. Eventually he heard the familiar whistle of the heron's damaged wing. Whistler landed beside him.

'Listen, Fox, excellent news,' said the heron. 'The men have gone indoors. The dog's chained up. The hens are back in the coop and the two dead chickens are hanging in a shed.'

Fox got up. 'Here's a chance,' he said. 'But what about the dog?'

'I think it's dozing,' Whistler replied. 'But go carefully.'

'I – I don't know if I can do it,' Fox said doubtfully. 'I'm not the strong, brave fox you like to remember me as. Winter and famine have altered me.'

'Try,' Whistler urged him. 'Think of Vixen. And the others too.'

30

Fox sighed and stared at the fence. Then he shook himself. 'All right,' he said. 'Here goes.'

Once more he jumped into the garden. Tawny Owl directed him to the shed. Fox padded slowly forward. The dog was clearly visible, lying half in and half out of its kennel. It was motionless. Fox wrenched the first chicken from its hook in the open shed and carefully plodded back to the fence where he dropped it. Then he returned. The second chicken was larger. Fox tugged hard but it wouldn't budge. With a particularly vicious wrench Fox pulled it away but in doing so knocked over some tools which made a clatter. The dog instantly awoke and began to bark again. Fox raced for the fence and leapt into the road. The three birds perched further along the fence. Badger was just returning and heard the dog. He rushed forward.

'Here,' snapped Fox. 'Take this!'

Badger grabbed the chicken while, in the teeth of danger, Fox made a supreme effort and was up and over the fence once more to collect the second one. He was soon by Badger's side again. The dog was beside itself with fury.

'Now, run!' Fox barked and set off towards the Park boundary. Badger lumbered after him, expecting any minute to have the massive dog on his heels. But nothing happened. The two animals stopped for a rest on the home side of the ditch. The birds perched nearby.

'Not – a bad – haul,' Fox summed up between pants.

'I don't understand – why we – weren't chased,' Badger gasped.

'Simple,' Fox replied. 'The men must have looked out and seen the coop with all the remaining hens safe inside. They never thought about the two dead ones being stolen. They think the dog did its duty this time.'

'Bravo, Fox,' Whistler said heartily. 'You're still a shade sharper than most.'

## CHAPTER SIX

When they got their breath back, Badger said, 'I found something else of great interest.'

'Food?' Kestrel enquired.

'Yes – all sorts,' Badger answered. 'Something for everyone. It's quite uncanny. It's all been dumped – at the end of the road.'

Fox shook his head. 'I'm sorry,' he said. 'I'm all in. You show the birds where it is, Badger. I'll stay here and guard the chickens.'

The road was now quiet but Badger took great care as he went along. At the end was a general store and it was the waste food stocks from this that Badger had discovered. There were vegetables, fruit and even nuts. The birds lost no time in collecting up what Badger thought would be most useful for his friends back in the Park. They looked a comical trio as they flew upwards clutching selections of greengrocery in their beaks and talons.

Badger rejoined Fox whose mouth was running with water in anticipation of the feast ahead.

'Come on, old friend,' said Badger. 'Let's get home and eat.'

Fox was so tired that it took the two animals some time to make the return journey over the snow. They took their chickens into Badger's sett and there Fox and Vixen, Badger and Weasel made an excellent meal. Some of the meat was left above ground for Owl and Kestrel who, with Whistler, were continuing to ferry supplies in from the dump for the smaller animals. By the next day, the Farthing Wood community had eaten better than for a long time and were feeling more cheerful. However the problem of finding regular supplies of meat for the larger animals remained.

The winter wore on and the new year came in without any change in the weather. The birds continued to make trips to the food dump and sometimes there was a little meat to be had. The animals had grown used to eating sparingly but at least now they knew they wouldn't starve. They were determined to last out the awful cold until spring arrived.

Winter was nearly at an end when a new threat came to White Deer Park. The Warden was ill and was suddenly taken away to hospital. Ginger Cat was taken in by a friend. Without the Warden, the Reserve was left unprotected.

It wasn't long before some humans found this out. One evening as Fox and Vixen were prowling they heard the sound of gunshot close at hand. Startled and frightened, they dived for cover. But they soon saw that they weren't the targets. Two men came into view carrying a large animal. Its lifeless body hung between them.

'A deer!' the foxes hissed together beneath their breath.

The men stumped away, obviously content with their haul.

'How can they do that?' Vixen raged. 'This is a protected area. Animals are supposed to be safe here.'

'Not while the Warden's away,' Fox remarked grimly.

'Oh, where can he have gone?' Vixen wailed. 'We're all at risk when people come here with guns.'

Sure enough, two days later another deer was killed. The smaller Park animals, though shocked, were relieved that it was the deer the killers wanted – for meat – as trophies – or for whatever purpose. But the deer herd was frantic. They had no experience of being hunted – they had always lived in the Nature Reserve where hunting was forbidden. Now the Park was a death-trap, for there was no means of escape.

Fox realized the deer needed help. The Farthing Wood animals were used to looking after one another and now that they shared White Deer Park as their home, they should help the others who were in such danger.

The men returned again and this time Fox and Vixen spotted them stalking the deer herd. The Great Stag towered over the other deer.

'They're going for *him* – I know it!' Fox cried and broke cover, barking an alarm.

The deer ran about nervously. Vixen joined in the alarm and all of the herd galloped off, some in one direction, some in another. A shot rang out. The Great Stag escaped, but another deer fell to the ground. She had run the wrong way – straight into the path of the poachers.

Fox blamed himself. 'I killed her. I drove her on to the guns,' he moaned.

Vixen was sharp. 'Of course you didn't kill her!' she snapped. 'What more could you have done? You warned them and saved the Stag. We can't defeat humans with guns.'

'We have to,' Fox insisted. 'We have to prevent these killers getting into the Park.'

'Impossible,' Vixen declared.

But Fox was determined. 'We must try to prevent this slaughter,' he said. 'I need to talk to the Great Stag.'

The leader of the deer herd hadn't gone far. He thanked Fox for his warning. Then he said, 'We only lost one. It could have been worse without you.'

'We have to think of a better way to fight the poachers,' said Fox.

The Stag shook his head. 'I fear there is nothing you can do,' he said. 'If the killing goes on, we deer have only one course of action. Somehow we must leave the Park and scatter outside.'

'Give me a little time,' Fox pleaded. 'Don't leave yet. The men don't come every night. I'll think of a plan.'

'Whatever you wish, Fox,' said the Stag. 'You have proved to be our friend.'

As Fox and Vixen turned away, Fox murmured, 'The Pond is the answer. I'll keep a close eye on it.'

Fox, like everyone, was longing for milder weather. But he had a special reason. And, gradually, it did get a little less cold. The hard snow softened and the ice on the Pond became thinner. This was what Fox had been waiting for.

The white deer were still in the Park. They had lost another of the herd and the Stag had begun to think again about leaving. Then Fox came to him and explained his plan. The Stag listened carefully.

'It's clever but risky,' he commented. 'However, Fox, we can only try it out.'

Fox next described his plan to Vixen. He wanted her approval. She looked at him with eyes that shone with admiration. She didn't need to speak. Fox was content.

'Now we have to get organized,' he said. 'We must arrange sentries.' He went to speak to his friends.

The animals were posted to watch the place where the poachers entered the Park. Tawny Owl, Kestrel and Whistler spread out along the fence. On the ground Hare, Badger and Vixen waited. Midway between the boundary and the Pond was Fox, while the Great Stag patrolled the edge of the Pond itself, ready to play his part.

On the first night there was no sign of the poachers. The watchers gave up at dawn. The next night

37

the sharp ears of the animals picked up steady human footsteps getting nearer. Tawny Owl was first to see the figures. She at once flew off to warn Fox.

The other birds and the animals kept the men in sight, moving a little ahead of them. Tawny Owl hooted to Fox, 'Run to the Pond! They're on their way.'

Fox raced to the Pond. 'Get ready!' he cried to the Stag. Then he turned and dashed back to find the men.

The three birds were perching safely out of sight in a popular tree. Hare swiftly took cover. Badger, Vixen and Weasel saw Fox coming towards them. 'Hide yourselves,' he panted.

Fox lay in wait for the men. As soon as he spotted their shadowy forms approaching he stood up and yapped loudly. At this signal the White Deer herd emerged from a nearby copse. The men stopped and pointed. Fox heard their rough voices. He knew they were looking amongst the deer for the herd's leader. Fox yapped again, running towards the deer. They scattered as they had been instructed, all cantering towards the Pond. The men shouted angrily as they saw the fox once again spoiling their hunt.

Fox ran behind the herd as though driving them. He steeled himself to keep on course. He knew he was risking death. His spine tingled and he glanced back. One of the men was raising his gun to take aim. Fox wheeled suddenly and began to run a zig-zag course. A shot cracked out but it was wasted.

The men broke into a run now. They didn't want the deer to escape. The herd reached the Pond and fanned out around its edge. Behind them the Great Stag stepped on to the ice and inched forward until he reached the limit of safety. As the men came up the herd swung away, leaving the solitary Stag exposed on the ice. The men couldn't believe their luck. They raised their guns again. But now Fox let out a fierce bark. The Stag gathered himself together and leapt to safety on the shore. The men swore but wouldn't give up. They pursued him blindly on to the ice, running forwards to take aim. Suddenly – crash! – the ice broke beneath them and they plunged down; down into the freezing water. Their guns were tossed away as they fought to save themselves. The men floundered, trying to get a handhold on something.

The Stag turned at the pond-edge and saw the guns sink to the murky depths of the Pond bottom. The great beast bellowed in triumph. Fox was surrounded by his jubilant friends.

'That,' boomed the Stag, 'is the finest piece of animal cunning I've ever witnessed.'

Meanwhile the men were striking out for the shore. Their cries of distress and misery found no sympathisers among the animals. They pulled themselves on to land, glaring towards the animals. Soaked to the skin and thoroughly chilled, the poachers set off at a run across the Park.

'I think we've seen the last of them,' said Hare. 'Fox, you've surpassed yourself.'

Only Vixen, fiercely proud of her mate as she was, feared for the consequences. Two humans, fooled and humiliated in this way by a fox, would surely seek revenge.

# CHAPTER SEVEN

Fox's courage and cunning made him the hero of White Deer Park. Twice now he had outwitted humans, and all his old confidence returned. He held his head high.

Vixen was delighted. 'You're your old self again,' she told him joyfully. She kept her fears bottled up.

The weather continued to improve. The snow melted bit by bit and, now that the ground was softer, squirrels could dig up their stores of nuts. Berries and seeds were easier to find too, which pleased the voles and fieldmice. Whistler, Kestrel and Tawny Owl could stop the tiring flights to and from the food dump.

But soon afterwards Vixen was proved right. Weasel spied the two men entering the Reserve once more. She didn't run since she recalled the lost guns and so believed the men were harmless. However, it was obvious from their movements that they were searching for something.

'Can't be deer this time,' Weasel muttered to herself. 'I wonder what – ' she broke off as she saw a fox trotting over an open patch of ground. It was not an animal she recognized. The men hastily pulled pistols from their pockets and fired at the creature. One missed, but the other man was too close to fail, and the fox rolled over and lay motionless. The men nudged it with their boots to make sure it was dead. Weasel's heart pounded. She must find Fox and Vixen. But she stayed long enough to see that the men didn't leave the Park at once, but carried on searching.

Fox and Vixen had heard the two distant cracks of the guns and were standing hesitantly near their earth. Vixen was terribly afraid. Then Weasel came running.

'It's the same two men,' she squealed, 'and they've got a new kind of gun. You must take cover underground. They – '

Another shot rang out.

The animals were horrified. Vixen whispered, 'They're after all the foxes. I dreaded this.'

'No.' Fox shook his head with staring eyes. 'It's me they're after. They want revenge for the trick I played on them. They'll kill every fox they see in the hope that one of them is me.'

Weasel nodded dumbly.

'Come, Fox,' Vixen begged him, 'we must take shelter.'

Half dazed, Fox allowed himself to be led underground. Weasel sped away.

'What have I done?' said Fox. 'Innocent creatures are being slaughtered because of me. Oh, what have I done?'

Vixen tried to calm him. 'Think more of what you have to do *now*,' she urged him. 'The gunshot will have driven most creatures into hiding, so the immediate risk has faded. You must use your wits again. That's our best hope.'

Fox was comforted a little. 'Dear Vixen, whatever would I do without you?' he murmured.

Fox was not the only animal putting his mind to a new plan, as he was soon to discover. The Great Stag had been doing some thinking too.

A couple of days later Mole was busy constructing some new tunnels. He poked his head out of one shaft and was nearly trampled by the Stag's hoof.

'I beg your pardon,' the Stag said. 'I didn't see you at first. I'm looking for your friend Fox.'

'I'll give you directions,' Mole squeaked and sent the Stag on his way to Fox and Vixen's earth. It was daylight, so the Stag found them in their den.

'Your efforts to help us seem to have put you in danger,' the Stag said to Fox. 'I've heard all about the humans' return and I've heard their guns. You helped us – now it's our turn to help you. We owe you some protection.'

'Protection?' Fox muttered. 'How do you mean?'

'If the men return again to kill, the deer herd will put itself between you and the humans,' explained the Stag. 'And I don't mean just to shield you. We shall charge them and drive them from the Park. I don't think they'll want to quarrel with a few dozen pairs of lowered antlers.'

'It's a very generous and brave offer,' commented Vixen.

'It is indeed,' said Fox. 'I'll arrange to post sentries again, so that we have early warning. I'm certain they'll return. These men are relentless.'

The next day at dusk the poachers were spotted. Word was passed back along the line to the Great Stag who quickly gathered his herd. The men were in an ugly mood, shooting at anything that moved. Fox watched the deer get into position, the antlered animals in the front rank. Suddenly in the air there was a piercing cry. It was Kestrel.

'Great news,' she shrieked. 'I've just spied the ginger cat by the cottage. That means the Warden's back!'

The deer, poised for a charge, held themselves back momentarily. Fox saw how they could turn Kestrel's news to their advantage. He ran to the Great Stag.

'Drive the men to the cottage,' he cried. 'We'll have them trapped!'

The Stag roared his approval and the deer herd broke into a run. Their hooves thundered over the ground. The men swung round and saw the forest of antlers as the beasts galloped towards them. They took to their heels, running as fast as they could. The deer cut off their retreat and drove them in an arc towards the Warden's home. One man tried to take aim as he ran. The shot rang out but hit nothing.

The sound of the gun and the stampeding hooves brought the Warden and the vet, who was with him, to the cottage doorway. Light from inside the house flooded out and lit up the two terrified human fugitives about to be engulfed by a white tide of deer.

The Great Stag roared again and the herd slithered to a halt. The men were buffeted to the ground. The Warden and the vet were amazed by the scene but quickly took charge. The poachers were disarmed and marched indoors. For an instant the Warden glanced back. The deer were behaving in their usual peaceful way and were already busy cropping at the brown tufts of grass exposed by the thaw.

'How extraordinary!' the Warden exclaimed to his friend. 'I could almost swear the animals deliberately drove the poachers here.'

Peace returned to White Deer Park. The Reserve was in the care of the Warden again and mild weather came as Winter finally released its grip. Toad emerged from hibernation and went to greet his friends. Kestrel, as usual, was first to see him. She flew down.

'It's good to see you, Kestrel,' said Toad. 'I hope everyone is well?'

'Not everyone,' Kestrel replied. 'There have been losses. The winter was the hardest any of us can remember.'

Toad looked shocked. 'Who then – who hasn't survived?' he asked uncertainly.

'Many of the voles and mice died – some rabbits and squirrels, too. Finding food was a great problem. All of us tried to help one another, but you'll see some changes. The survivors are as lean as can be.'

'Well, there's plenty of food around now,' Toad said. 'They'll be able to fatten up.'

Fox and Vixen greeted Toad warmly. Early spring sunshine bathed them in its glow. 'Soon be time for Adder to rejoin us,' Fox remarked. 'Then our party will be complete again.'

The Farthing Wood animals decided to celebrate the end of winter in their usual meeting-place, the Hollow. When Adder was about again, the animals and birds gathered together. Their numbers were fewer than before the winter but the party was light-hearted. Each of them was united by a cosy feeling of friendship.

'This is a wonderful day,' said Whistler joyfully.

'Dear friends,' said Fox, 'let's make it one we shall always remember. Whatever may happen in the future, whatever fate may await us, we shall remember that this day, together, we rejoiced to say that WE ARE ALIVE.'

Part II

# FOX'S FEUD

# CHAPTER ONE

Later that spring an important event took place in White Deer Park. Vixen gave birth to four cubs, two male and two female. An excited Mole brought the news to Badger early one morning.

'Well, well, I must go and see them,' Badger said enthusiastically.

The proud father greeted his friend. 'We're so thrilled,' said Fox. 'Come along.'

Badger beamed. Inside the earth Vixen was curled up on a bed of soft hair. The four cubs nestled against her. The kindly Badger melted at the sight. 'A happy occasion indeed,' he murmured. 'May they have a more peaceful life than we have known.'

Vixen smiled. 'Thank you, dear Badger.'

The cubs grew steadily and Badger was a frequent visitor. He was amused by the little animals' antics. One of the male cubs seemed more advanced than the others.

'He'll be their leader,' Badger remarked shrewdly.

Vixen nodded. 'He takes after his father.'

They were interrupted by the arrival of Weasel. 'There's a strange fox snooping around outside,' she told them. 'He's a big animal with a long scar down his muzzle.'

Fox looked grim. 'I've seen him around,' he remarked. 'I don't like the look of him.'

'What's he after?' Badger wondered.

'I'm not sure,' Fox answered. 'He's always lived in the Park and he's the father of many of the young foxes here. I think he may feel Vixen and I are intruders on his territory.'

'Are we newcomers resented, do you think?' Badger asked.

'I believe some of the Park's inhabitants feel this is more their home than ours,' Weasel replied.

'Perhaps we should tread warily for a while,' Fox suggested. 'I'm going to ask Tawny Owl to keep an eye on the den when I'm out hunting. Meanwhile it might be a good idea for all of us to remain in our corner of the Park and respect the territories of those who were here before us.'

The cubs were soon old enough to play in the sunshine outside the earth. Tawny Owl took her turn at watching over them. One day, Vixen told the bird she and Fox had named three of the cubs.

'This one we call Charmer,' she said, pointing to one of the female cubs. 'She has winning little ways. And her sister is Dreamer.'

'Very apt,' Owl commented. 'She seems content to sit and bask.'

'The big male cub is Bold,' Vixen continued.

At that moment the fourth cub wandered over to

50

Tawny Owl, sniffed her all over whilst wagging his tail, then lay down across her feet with a deep sigh.

'I think this one's just named himself,' Owl remarked pleasantly. 'I shall call him Friendly.'

And there was no disagreement.

At dusk Tawny Owl awoke from a sleep with a start. The familiar shape of the scarfaced fox was skulking in the shadows. The animal paused at one of the entrances to Fox's earth, his head cocked as he listened carefully. His long muzzle sniffed at the scents around the den. Then he moved slowly off into the darkness.

After a while Fox emerged from inside. 'Are you there, Owl?' he called.

'Yes.' Owl landed beside him.

'Have you seen anything?'

'Yes. Scarface was around.'

'I knew it. I smelt him.'

'He must have found *your* scent,' said Owl, 'and decided to retreat.'

'I think so too. Had I been out hunting . . .'

'I'm sure I and Vixen could have dealt with him,' Tawny Owl declared stoutly.

'Hm.' Fox looked thoughtful. 'Perhaps Badger could help too. Scarface is a big animal. And I don't know what he's up to.'

'It could be curiosity,' Owl remarked. 'His own mate has produced three cubs and he may be simply interested in comparing them with yours.'

'We shall see,' said Fox.

And see they did. The next night Tawny Owl and Badger positioned themselves – the bird in a branch of a willow tree, Badger at the foot of it. Fox set off to go hunting. He gave no sign that he knew his friends were there. It was a bright moonlit night, clear and crisp.

For a while all was quiet, save only for the faint rustle of an evening breeze through the dead leaves. Then Badger tensed as he heard the pitter patter of cautious footsteps. A long shadow was cast over the silvery ground as Scarface came into view, treading slowly. He went straight to the entrance of Fox's den, then paused to look around in case he was followed. He saw nothing, but Badger saw plenty. The beast's face was scarred and hideous from many a battle. It was grim and fierce and threatening. Badger's brave heart missed a beat. Scarface turned away and lowered himself to enter the hole.

At once Owl and Badger rushed forward.

'Not so fast,' Owl screeched. 'What's your game?'

Scarface started and snarled, angry at being discovered. 'Who are you to ask?' he barked.

'Someone who has been asked to keep watch for intruders,' Owl replied.

'Intruders?' snapped Scarface. 'Intruders? How dare you talk to me of intruders – me, Scarface, who has lived all his life in this Park.'

'Just because you were born here doesn't mean you own the Park,' said Badger. 'What right have you got to enter another fox's earth?'

'I've more right in this earth than he has,' Scarface

growled. 'Oh, I know all about you newcomers and your heroic journey from Farthing Wood,' he went on sarcastically. 'I saw you all arrive, just like everyone else. That was one thing. But now you've started breeding . . .'

'*We* haven't,' Badger corrected him. 'Owl and I, we have no mates. And in any case, you've nothing to fear from any of our party. We want no trouble.'

'You have to eat. You're competition for me and my kind.'

'There's plenty of room for everyone,' said Badger.

Scarface bristled with anger. 'Oh no, not for everyone,' he snarled menacingly. 'The whole of this Reserve is my hunting territory. My ancestors lived and hunted here long before humans fenced it off and gave it a name. And my cubs will hunt here after me. But as for your friend the Farthing Wood fox and his family – the real intruders – tell them to stay in their own quarter if they value their safety. I shall be watching and I don't shrink from fighting!' Scarface finished with a snarl and loped off into the darkness.

'Dear, dear,' muttered Badger. 'What an unpleasant character.'

When Fox returned, Badger and Owl told him of the unpleasant visitor.

'We spoilt his plan all right,' said Owl. 'I'm sure he was about to do some mischief to your cubs.'

Fox looked solemn. 'I shall do exactly as he asks,'

he said firmly. 'I must put Vixen and the cubs first – I won't have them at risk.'

'Quite right, Fox,' Badger agreed. 'He's a vicious-looking beast if ever I saw one.'

'Don't tell Vixen of this,' Fox asked. 'I'll let her know all she needs to.'

'Well, Fox, remember you can rely on us. We're always here to help,' Badger said.

'That is a great comfort,' Fox replied. 'Thank you – both of you.'

The friends parted.

# CHAPTER TWO

The time came for the cubs' first hunting lesson. Vixen led them from the den. Many of the Farthing Wood animals had gathered to watch the event.

'Don't forget,' Fox said to his mate. 'Keep within our home area.'

Vixen nodded. 'Don't worry,' she replied. 'I know the rules.'

The cubs followed her closely. Bold was eager and excited, and occasionally ran ahead until Vixen called him back. Friendly, Charmer and Dreamer dogged their mother's heels. She took them to the stream-side where there were plenty of water-voles and shrews. She began to show the cubs how to stalk and pounce on prey. From a distance Fox kept an eye on them. He wanted to be quite sure there was no danger.

Bold was the quickest to learn. He caught a shrew and was praised by his mother. 'You're getting the hang of it,' she told him. 'Dreamer, you're not pay-ing enough attention. Friendly, Charmer, you need more patience.'

Unknown to the fox family, an envious onlooker was hiding in the undergrowth on the opposite bank. Scarface glared at the sturdy cubs, in particular Bold who seemed already confident and skilful. He thought of his own cubs who were at that moment with their mother, learning the same skills. How puny they appeared by comparison! Scarface watched Bold with murder in his heart. He saw the youngsters as a threat and decided that the threat had to be removed.

When her cubs' lesson was over, Vixen led them homeward. Fox heaved a sigh of relief that all had gone well and trotted away. But Scarface barked suddenly, startling the cubs.

'Quickly, run home!' Vixen cried. 'As fast as you can.'

Scarface raced forward swiftly and cut off Bold. The other cubs scattered. But Bold stood his ground as the fierce animal cornered him. When Scarface attacked, Bold skipped aside and actually nipped his enemy on the foreleg. Scarface was so surprised by Bold that he even fell back a pace. This gave Vixen a chance to protect Bold, snapping at the enemy fox furiously, as Scarface tried to attack again. More help arrived as Bold's father joined in. Scarface saw that he was outnumbered and slipped away. Meanwhile Badger and some other friends went to see the other cubs safely home.

'Bold's all right,' Vixen assured Fox. 'He's a brave little creature. Do you know, he dared to bite that scarfaced brute?'

Fox swelled with pride. 'Well, how about that?'

'I had to defend myself,' Bold said calmly. 'Where are the others?'

'Back in the den, I hope,' Fox answered. 'Scarface has proved himself false. We kept to our side of the bargain, but he still attacked. At least we know now where we stand.'

Just then Badger lumbered up. 'The other two are safely home,' he announced. Then he noticed only Bold was with his parents. 'But where's Dreamer?'

'Isn't she with the others?' cried Vixen.

'No. I thought she was with you,' Badger replied.

Fox took control. 'Badger, you take Bold back. Vixen, you go that way. I'll go this. We must find Dreamer.'

They raced in different directions. Then Vixen heard Fox give a cry – an angry howl of distress. She ran towards him and found him standing by the body of her cub. Poor Dreamer had been savagely killed and there was only one animal who could have done it – Scarface.

Fox vowed with a snarl, 'He will pay for this.'

The Farthing Wood animals were all shocked by the brutal killing of the pretty young cub. Some thought she should be avenged; others advised caution.

Vixen's grief was deep and Fox itched for battle. However, he didn't want to make the Park an even more dangerous home for his remaining three cubs, so he held back.

Eventually the cubs were able to hunt on their own. Friendly and Charmer were content to stay within the home territory, but Bold was keen to explore further. He told his brother and sister not to breathe a word to their father.

Filled with a sense of freedom and adventure, Bold set off in the moonlight entirely alone. He wasn't afraid of anything. He ran to the stream and looked across. He had never before dared to cross to the other side. He entered the water and dog-paddled over. He was excited to find that everywhere there were new sights and smells.

'Hallo,' hissed a voice nearby. 'I don't think I know your face.'

Bold looked around. A snake was coiled under a gorse bush. 'Hallo,' he replied. 'You must be Adder.'

'The same,' she said.

'I'm Bold.'

'You are indeed,' Adder answered. 'Your parents don't hunt on this side of the stream. Are you sure you are wise to stray here? Look what happened to your sister.'

'Dreamer was on our side of the stream, but it didn't save her,' Bold pointed out. 'Why should we be confined then?'

'No reason,' Adder admitted. 'Feel free to go. Don't let me hold you back.'

Bold paused. 'I'm grateful for your advice,' he said politely. 'If I don't return tonight, will you find my father and tell him?'

Adder hesitated. She didn't like to commit herself. But she felt true loyalty towards Fox. 'All right,' she said at length.

Bold thanked her and trotted forward again. Pretty soon he detected the smell of a strange fox.

58

He halted. Another young fox came into view. It was moving just as cautiously as Bold. It spotted him and sat down nervously. It didn't look as strong as Bold.

'I mean no harm,' Bold said. 'I'm only looking around.'

'You shouldn't be looking around here,' the other cub answered. 'We don't allow strangers on our territory. You must be a Farthing Wood fox.'

'Oh no,' Bold corrected him. 'I'm as much a White Deer Park fox as you are. I was born here too, you know.'

The other cub was silenced by this remark.

'What's your name?' Bold asked, trying to be friendly.

'Ranger.'

'I'm Bold. Now tell me, why do we have to quarrel? We might be friends elsewhere. Why not here?'

Ranger was encouraged. He moved closer but, before he could respond, his father appeared abruptly. Scarface snarled viciously at Bold.

'This will be the first and last time you enter our territory.'

Bold stood firm, awaiting the attack he knew was bound to come. Ranger looked unhappy. He didn't seem to know what was expected of him. Scarface flung himself on Bold who neatly sidestepped him. The elder fox's rush carried him on a little distance. Bold profited by this and turned tail.

'Come on, come on,' Scarface snapped at his son. 'Don't just stand there. Pursue him!'

Bold was far too swift-footed for either Ranger or his father to catch him. He exulted in his speed, sure of his escape. Then he heard an eerie cry – half-yelp and half-scream. The cry was repeated. Scarface was calling for assistance.

Bold put on speed, but ahead of him his path was suddenly blocked. Several foxes were running to encircle him. Scarface's cries of triumph rang in his ears. Bold was surrounded. He looked from one pair of eyes to another. They showed no signs of mercy.

# CHAPTER THREE

When the first light of day filtered through to the Park, Adder knew she must report Bold's absence. The difficulty was, she was a long way from Fox and Vixen's earth and she was a slow traveller. She needed to pass the message to a fleet-footed runner. She was lucky to find Hare lying in the grass.

'Bold's in trouble,' Adder hissed. 'On the wrong side of the stream. He's a headstrong youngster. You must alert Fox straight away.'

Hare galloped away with Adder's message. He found Fox and Vixen were already worried about Bold's disappearance.

'If he's entered Scarface's territory we may be too late,' Fox said. 'But we must go at once.'

'I'll round up the others,' Hare offered.

'No.' Fox shook his head determinedly. 'This is our family's quarrel and ours alone. You and the other animals must keep out of it. Thank you for bringing the news, Hare.'

Fox, Vixen, Friendly and Charmer (now nearly full grown) set off for the stream at top speed. Meanwhile Hare, despite Fox's wishes, decided to fetch Badger, Owl, Kestrel and Weasel. He thought there could be no harm in their following behind in case they were needed.

Badger didn't want to interfere. 'We'll just shadow them,' he said. They swam the stream, the birds flying above.

'Here,' Owl called down. 'A bank of nettles. You could hide in there while Kestrel and I go on ahead.'

The animals had just settled themselves when they were astonished to see Bold, the cause of all the trouble, running from another direction toward the stream.

Badger called his name and the group ran out to check him.

'I escaped,' Bold panted. A shoulder was bleeding. 'I'm too fast for them. There was a bit of a scuffle. I'll have to take a breather . . . and then I'll explain.'

The animals waited patiently. Bold recovered his breath. 'I was ambushed by Scarface's tribe. They took me to a deserted earth and forced me inside. Luckily, most had been out in search of prey so only a couple were left to guard me while the others went back to their hunting. I tricked one fox to come inside the earth and, after a tussle, I escaped. I ducked the other guard's attack and then simply ran and ran. And here I am.' Bold looked very pleased with himself.

'You're a very lucky cub,' Badger told him. 'But you've been thoughtless. Your family have gone in search of you and could well be in greater danger now than you were.'

Bold's high spirits were dashed. 'Oh, I didn't

mean this to happen,' he wailed. 'I must go to help them!'

'You'll stay where you are,' Badger ordered him sternly. 'We'll wait for Kestrel and Owl to report their findings.'

The birds returned quite soon. 'Vixen, Charmer and Friendly are safe,' Kestrel announced. 'They've been released by Scarface in exchange for Fox being their prisoner.' She and Owl were amazed to see the careless Bold sitting there calmly.

'What nonsense is this?' Owl asked him severely.

Bold hung his head, ashamed of his stupidity. Before he could reply, his mother, brother and sister were spotted running swiftly towards the stream. They were relieved to find Bold almost unharmed, but Vixen's relief turned to anger as Badger explained what had happened.

'I hope this will teach you to think about others as well as yourself,' she snapped at Bold. 'Look what your foolishness has caused. Your father is in real danger!'

'Vixen, take your family home,' Badger said with all the authority of Fox's deputy. 'And Hare, Weasel, there's nothing you can do either. I shall go to Fox's aid. I'm known as a reasonable sort of creature. And Fox's wits have got him out of tight corners before. I'm sure, between us, we can save the situation.'

Owl and Kestrel flew back to the scene of Fox's surrender and Badger lumbered after them. Badger was quite unprepared for what he found.

Fox was sitting, perfectly calmly, under a pine tree on which Owl and Kestrel were perching. Facing him at a short distance were Scarface and many of his tribe of foxes. The space in between was occupied by the Great Stag who was addressing all of them.

'There's no doubt that all the inhabitants of the Reserve owe something to the Farthing Wood animals – and Fox in particular – for the courageous way in which they rid us all of the threat of poachers during the winter.'

Scarface growled, 'Not without making some of my tribe targets for the humans.'

'Our herd, too, lost several of our members to their guns,' the Stag reminded him. 'Had it not been for Fox's planning, there could have been far more deaths.'

Scarface was silent. The Stag was the most important animal in the Park and no one challenged that. There could be no arguments. Fox saw that he could go and, thanking the Stag, joined Badger. The two animals left quickly and Owl and Kestrel followed.

'How did the Stag come to be in the area?' Badger asked. 'Was it just a coincidence?'

'I don't know. It was uncanny,' Fox replied. 'But Scarface won't be satisfied by my escape. You can be sure he'll be plotting something to get even. We must all be on our guard more than ever.'

Badger told Fox about Bold. 'Yes, Owl explained,' said Fox. 'I think the young scamp has learnt his lesson.'

In the midst of some thick vegetation, Adder reared up in their path. She had a knowing look on her face. Badger put two and two together.

'Here's the creature who put the Stag on your trail, I'll be bound,' he chuckled.

Adder leered but said nothing.

'Adder, I'm greatly in your debt,' said Fox. 'And not for the first time. Where can we find you if we need you again?'

'I shall be within walking distance,' the snake answered. And that was all they could get out of her.

## CHAPTER FOUR

It wasn't more than a day or two before Scarface found a way to strike back at the Farthing Wood animals. On a breezy day he found Hare's mate crouching on her form. There was no chance of any warning, because the killer's scent was blown away by the wind. The harmless beast was slaughtered without a sound. Hare and his youngster, Leveret, poured out their anger and grief to Fox.

'We must get rid of this threat,' Fox declared, 'and soon. Scarface is a clever, cunning animal and it will require stealth. He musn't suspect anything. There's only one creature, to my mind, who can catch him unawares.'

'Adder?' Hare guessed.

'Exactly. Her poison will do the job. But she won't do it if she thinks she's being ordered. It will need a suggestion for her to take up the idea. And this is where Bold can redeem himself. He admires Adder and she knows it. I think he's the one to put the idea in her head.'


Bold, of course, was delighted to be given this

mission. But Friendly begged to be allowed to go with his brother and finally Fox gave in.

'All right,' he said, 'but let Bold do most of the talking.'

Just after dawn the next day the two cubs set out. They went towards the place amongst long grass and bracken where they expected the snake to be.

'Supposing we can't find her anywhere?' Friendly wondered.

'Oh, if Adder's around, she's sure to be keeping an eye open for everyone's comings and goings,' Bold answered. 'She's so alert.'

'Are you referring to me?' came a familiar drawl. And Adder slithered into view.

'Oh! Yes!' Bold cried, a little surprised. 'My parents send their regards.'

'Please return them,' Adder replied graciously. 'Do you – er – need me for something?' she added mischievously as she saw the cubs showed no sign of moving on.

'Another of our friends has been killed,' Friendly blurted out. 'Hare's mate was the victim. Father thinks we have to take action.'

Adder saw how the land lay. 'And the Farthing Wood community must band together to do this?' she asked slyly.

'No, not all of them. Only one,' Friendly gabbled. Bold glowered at him.

'Oh-ho, I see,' Adder grinned. 'I'm to be the tool to carry out the job?'

'Why didn't you keep quiet?' Bold snapped at his

brother. They had no hope of just suggesting their idea now.

'Oh dear,' Adder leered. 'A slight disagreement.'

'I should have come alone,' Bold growled. Friendly looked uncomfortable.

'No matter,' Adder hissed. 'You may tell your father that I shall do all in my power to even the score. And it's been a pleasure talking to you,' she went on. 'Remember, you don't need an excuse to come visiting me.' She slid away, barely rustling the grass-stems as she went.

Friendly crowed, 'We did it! We did it, Bold!'

But his brother wasn't so confident that they had carried out their father's scheme exactly as required. 'Adder guessed we'd been sent deliberately,' he muttered. 'She's so sly. But we won't let on. Scarface will be killed and that's all that matters.'

He was to find later that he had made a costly mistake, one that he would regret for a very long time.

It was Whistler the heron who discovered there had been a mistake. Whilst fishing upstream he noticed a young fox – one of Scarface's brood – showing signs of distress. It was moaning and lurching about unsteadily. As Whistler watched, the fox's legs gave way and it fell on its side, body heaving and twitching.

'Looks like snakebite,' Whistler said to himself.

The fox shuddered and lay still. Whistler flew over to take a closer look. The animal was dead. 'This isn't Scarface, but it's Adder's work, surely.

68

Why did she strike the wrong fox?' He flew quickly to bring the news.

The Farthing Wood animals soon found out how Bold and Friendly had failed to give the correct message.

'How could Adder know what was expected of her if you didn't even mention Scarface by name?' Fox demanded furiously.

The cubs hung their heads. 'We – we thought –' Bold stammered.

'Never mind what you thought,' Tawny Owl snapped. 'Adder's risked herself for nothing and, if we know anything about Scarface, he'll be on her trail. He'll suspect the Farthing Wood Adder rather than another snake.'

When Adder herself found how she had attacked the wrong animal, she was angry, but not with the cubs. 'I should have realized what was required of me,' she said to Fox. 'The youngsters are not wholly to blame. I'll lie low.' She made up her own mind to make good her mistake when she had the chance. But she didn't tell anyone about this.

Meanwhile the Farthing Wood animals kept guard every night for the expected attack from Scarface. As for Scarface himself, he knew Adder was his enemy and was determined to make sure he hunted her out. She wouldn't be the first snake to have her life brought to a sudden end by his powerful jaws. Scarface was quite aware that Fox was posting guards night after night to warn of his coming. He chuckled grimly to himself. 'Nothing will happen while there are guards around. I'm too old a hand to be caught like that!' And the Park was quiet.

'Why not let the cubs take their turn at keeping watch?' Vixen suggested to Fox. 'The experience will be useful to them.'

'It'll give us a rest too,' Fox agreed.

One night whilst Bold was on guard duty, his brother and sister had gone their separate ways to hunt. Charmer had run farther afield. On her way home she became aware she was being followed. She stopped and saw a pair of eyes glinting in the moonlight. They belonged to another fox cub.

'I've seen you before,' said the cub, a male.

'Yes. And I recognize you,' said Charmer. 'You're one of Scarface's young ones.'

'I'm Ranger. Once I talked to your brother Bold. What are you called?'

'Charmer.'

'I can see why.'

Charmer was surprised. 'I – I'm on my way home,' she murmured.

'Couldn't we talk awhile?' Ranger asked. 'The quarrel's between our parents, not us.'

'We have to remain loyal to our families,' Charmer replied. Ranger didn't answer. But he continued to follow her.

'My brothers may come looking for me,' Charmer warned him. Secretly, though, she was flattered.

'Well, perhaps we may meet another time,' Ranger said regretfully. 'I often come to this spot. You'll know the way now, I think.'

'I make no promises,' Charmer replied. But she already knew she would return.

Further on, Friendly came to meet her. 'I've been searching for you,' he said. 'Were you lucky in your hunting?'

'Very,' Charmer murmured with a secret smile.

Friendly looked at her sharply. There was something different about her.

The next night it was Friendly's turn to guard. Bold and Charmer hunted on their own. Charmer went straight to the area where she had met Ranger the night before. He was there, with some prey he had caught for her. He wagged his tail in greeting. 'These are for you.' He offered her some dead shrews and water-rats.

'Thank you,' she said warmly and ate.

'I know where we can catch some more,' said Ranger.

'I don't think we should hunt together,' Charmer replied. 'We might run into Bold or – worse still – my father.'

'Would it matter? We mean no harm.'

'I'm sure my family wouldn't see it that way.'

Her words were hardly out of her mouth when a low growl was heard nearby. Charmer vanished as Bold suddenly raced into the clearing. He didn't see her. The two male cubs sized each other up.

'You've filled out a bit since we last met,' said Bold. He could see, though, that Ranger was still no match for him. 'Well, I've no wish to fight you.'

'Why do we need to be enemies?' Ranger asked.

'Ha! Your father will explain that to you,' Bold muttered. 'Well, goodbye for now.' He trotted away.

On his way home Bold paused to speak to Friendly. 'Have you seen our sister?'

'Oh yes, I've seen her.' Friendly smiled. 'And she's never looked better.'

## CHAPTER FIVE

For days Adder remained in hiding close to the stream. She was waiting for Scarface to come close to her lair. The snake deliberately starved herself so that her store of venom wasn't used in killing to eat. She could go without food for days without harm, but she did want warmth. Unfortunately, there was a cool period of weather and when at last the sun shone again, Adder knew she must come out to warm her reptile blood. It was no good feeling sluggish when the enemy might appear at any moment.

She found a space amongst some ferns where she could feel the sun without wriggling into the open. And here she was lying when Ranger, chasing a rabbit, spotted her. He hurried home to tell his father.

Scarface listened to his son. 'It could hardly be the snake we're seeking,' he said. 'That one's far too secretive to be sunbathing in full view.'

But later, after some thought, Scarface decided to catch the adder by surprise. 'One snake less – whatever one it is – would be no bad thing.'

Silently, he approached the spot Ranger had described. He saw the snake and burst upon her. Adder wriggled to one side, avoiding Scarface's snapping jaws. Then a chase began as Adder took flight from the fox's surprise attack. In a straight fight she would have no chance, and even in the chase Scarface's jaws snapped this way and that. It was only a matter of time before they would close on the snake's body. Luckily Adder found a bolt-hole and she shot into it – but not quite quickly enough. Scarface's teeth gripped the end of her tail and a horrible tug-of-war began. During the struggle a chunk of Adder's tail was bitten right through. The snake escaped but was wounded.

Deep in the burrow, she nursed her wound. The pain was awful. Scarface spat out the segment of tail and roared down the hole, 'You miserable worm! Did you think you could outwit Scarface like any ordinary fox?'

Adder didn't admit to the previous killing. 'You can wait there till you drop with hunger,' she hissed painfully. 'You'll never outlast me. I shall stay here until I die if necessary.'

Scarface skulked around the bolt-hole, seething with fury. He knew there was no way he could reach Adder and that he would have to give her up for now. He still didn't know if had got the guilty snake and, if not, the real fox-killer was slithering free.

After a while Adder knew she had been left alone. She coiled around in the hole so that she could see the daylight outside. She felt bitter towards all foxes, whose quarrel had caused her to suffer this severe wound. For the rest of her days she would bear Scarface's mark on her body. And, as she thought of that, she began to plot again. This time she had been caught napping, but it wasn't in her nature to go un-avenged. Scarface would pay for this day's work.

Meanwhile Ranger continued to meet Charmer every night. No-one knew of these meetings except Friendly who, true to his name, saw no harm in them and didn't give his sister away.

But a difficulty arose when Charmer was asked to take her turn at guard duty. She had no way of in-forming Ranger she wouldn't be able to meet him.

'Can't I keep watch tomorrow night, Father?' she asked Fox with concern.

'No. Tomorrow I shall be watching,' he replied. 'I want to hunt tonight.'

Charmer took up her station, wondering all the while what Ranger might do. During the night she found out. He came looking for her. Charmer's heart sank as she saw him approach. He had picked up her scent and had followed the trail right on to the Farthing Wood territory. He saw Charmer and ran forward.

'Where have you been?' he cried. 'I waited and waited. Why are you – '

'Sssh!' She cut him short. 'You're out of bounds. My father and brothers are hunting and may return any moment. You must leave!'

'But why didn't you come?' Ranger pleaded.

'I can't explain now. But please, Ranger, go!'

'I'm no threat,' Ranger protested. 'Bold and I have met before. We understand each other.'

'You *don't* understand,' Charmer wailed. 'If he

75

finds you *here* – ' She broke off as, with a gulp, she saw Bold trotting homeward.

Bold picked up Ranger's scent, swung round and saw the strange cub. He barked angrily and rushed over.

'You've come too far this time,' he growled. 'Charmer, go back to the den.'

'No. No. Let him go, Bold,' Charmer cried. 'Ranger came in friendship.'

'Friendship?' Bold scoffed. 'With an enemy?'

'I'm no enemy to you,' Ranger declared. 'I came in peace to talk to your sister.'

'What?' Bold snapped. 'So, Charmer, you invite our enemy into our territory? This is how you guard us!'

'She didn't invite me,' Ranger explained. 'Charmer didn't know I would come.'

'She gave no alarm call, though,' Bold said. 'Why not? How can we trust you, Charmer?'

Friendly now arrived on the scene and immediately guessed what had happened. 'Bold, come away a moment,' he said. 'There's something you need to know.'

Bold was even more angry when Friendly had described Charmer's relationship with Ranger. He rushed back and leapt at Ranger. 'Leave my sister alone!' he snarled.

Charmer tried to intervene. Then Fox and Vixen arrived in the midst of the struggle.

'Stop!' Fox ordered. 'What is happening here?'

'Charmer is trying to defend an enemy against her own brother,' Bold barked furiously.

'No, no,' Charmer protested. 'I want no fighting over me.'

Friendly said, 'Charmer and Ranger are friends, Father. Bold objects to this.'

Fox looked long and hard at the cubs. 'You are one of Scarface's offspring,' he said to Ranger. 'And yet you are a friend of my daughter's?'

'Charmer and I met by chance some while ago,' Ranger replied. 'And – and – '

'And I left you on guard,' Fox interrupted, turning to Charmer. 'Why is he here?'

'He came looking for me, because I wasn't at our meeting place,' Charmer answered.

'Oh. Now I understand.' Fox nodded. 'Well, this needs thinking about.' He didn't sound too pleased.

Vixen said soothingly, 'There's no harm done. Ranger, you must return home now.'

'To tell his father we keep watch for him every night?' Bold objected hotly.

'I shall tell him nothing,' Ranger answered. 'I want no battles.' With a sad glance at Charmer he turned away.

Fox watched him uncertainly. Vixen nuzzled her mate. 'These things happen, my love,' she said gently. 'It's just that we were unprepared.'

## CHAPTER SIX

Scarface had a grudge against the Farthing Wood animals. It seemed to him that all his troubles started from the time they entered the Reserve. In particular he hated Fox. He brooded and in his dark heart the only solution seemed to be to destroy every one of the band. When Ranger returned he found his father surrounded by his tribe, and Scarface was spelling out his plans. Ranger slunk to the back of the group and listened in horror.

'I can wait no longer. These creatures are a threat to us all as long as they live. So there's one way out for us – destroy them, all of them. We'll attack them in daylight when they are unguarded. We shall strike like lightning. Is that understood?'

There was not a murmur.

'In two days, then,' said Scarface, 'we assemble here. Now go and prepare yourselves.'

The group broke up. Ranger knew he must save Charmer. But how? He could hardly fight against his own tribe. NO, there was only one thing to do. Somehow he must prevent this battle.

He thought first of warning Charmer the next night at their meeting-place. Then he realized she might be prevented from coming, now that her family knew about their meetings. Ranger only cared for Charmer. He wasn't concerned for her brothers or her father, and he knew nothing about the foxes' friendship and protection of the smaller and weaker Farthing Wood animals. He realized his only hope was to make his father change his mind.

Scarface, of course, wouldn't listen to any argument. He was determined to wipe out Fox and his friends, blinded as Scarface was by his jealousy and loathing.

'You're no son of mine,' the horrible animal growled at Ranger. 'Such a weakling! I wish I had *his* offspring and he mine.'

Ranger was beaten. But he still intended to prevent Charmer coming to harm, whatever else might happen.

But Scarface – and Ranger – had quite overlooked one advantage the Farthing Wood animals had – that was the keen gaze of Kestrel who patrolled the skies over the Park by day, missing nothing. When she saw movement around Scarface's territory she dropped down and found the foxes massing behind their leader. Swift as an arrow she sped to warn her friends.

'Go into your burrows!' she screeched to the rabbits. 'There's trouble coming.'

'Scarface?'

'Yes. I'll send the hares to you.'

Kestrel flew on to Fox's earth. 'This is it,' she shrilled. 'Scarface's foxes are coming in force!'

Fox acted at once. Owl was told to round up the mice and voles and send them to Badger's sett. Then Vixen led her three cubs to the same safe haven. Fox ran to find Weasel and the hedgehogs.

'Go to Badger's sett. No time to waste,' he told them. 'Squirrels, get into the trees!' he called. 'And stay there.'

Fox ran for cover too. But once in Badger's sett he saw three friends were missing – Mole, Toad and Adder.

'Mole will have the sense to stay in his tunnels,' Badger assured him. 'And Toad has the pond for cover.'

'And Adder?'

'No-one has seen her.'

'Very well,' said Fox. 'Kestrel has probably saved the day.'

Scarface was puzzled by the stillness around them as the foxes advanced. When he saw Kestrel wheeling high above, a crafty grin stole over his face. 'Aha, there's our explanation,' he muttered. 'Well, it seems we may have some digging to do.'

He led his band towards Fox's earth. Ranger, noting their direction, ran on ahead. He could think only of warning Charmer. He dived into the earth. Of course the den was empty.

'There's no-one inside,' he reported with relief.

'No-one?' growled Scarface. 'Well, since you're so keen, Ranger, you follow their scent. See where they've gone.'

Ranger was disappointed but then realized he

could turn this to his advantage. He would lead Scarface off the scent and away from Charmer's hideout. But Scarface wasn't to be put off. After a while he roared out, 'Where are you taking us? We're no nearer discovering them!'

He put another cub on the trail who was unable to pick up any scent at all.

'Useless, all of you!' Scarface seethed and cast about angrily. He detected movement nearby. The soil erupted and Mole, inquisitive as ever, stuck his head out.

'Now!' Scarface cried. 'You can help!'

'Me?' muttered Mole.

'Yes, you can take a message to your Farthing Wood friends,' Scarface growled. 'And the message is this!' He lunged at the little animal. Mole only just escaped Scarface's jaws. He dug himself down as deep as he could go.

'Dig him out, dig him out!' Scarface bellowed.

But foxes were no match for a mole in tunnelling, and the little creature was soon into the passage leading to Badger's sett.

'You can't track, you can't dig, you're worse than useless,' Scarface cursed his followers. 'I hope for your sakes you can fight!'

Mole tumbled into the midst of his friends, shrilling excitedly, 'Scarface attacked me! He's got all his tribe with him. We'll be trapped here!'

Badger quickly examined his little friend to make sure he hadn't been hurt. 'We won't be trapped,

81

Mole,' he comforted him. 'We can defend ourselves, we're all together in this.'

'We're outnumbered,' Mole said. 'You haven't seen them all.'

Fox took Badger aside. 'We have to face the fact,' he said, 'that there are only six of us who can defend the rest. You, me, Vixen, Bold, Friendly and Charmer – brave though they are, the others aren't up to fighting foxes.'

'We must post the strongest animals at each of the four entrances to the sett,' said Badger.

'Yes,' Fox agreed. 'Our only hope is to pick off the enemy one by one, for only one of them can enter at a time.'

'I'll go to the main exit to see how close they are,' Badger offered.

The enemy was almost on them. Badger was doubtful about their chances.

'Keep silent, everyone,' Fox hissed. 'They may pass us by.'

But the words had hardly passed his lips when there was a scuffling noise at the entrance. The animals knew that an enemy was approaching. They heard a voice.

'Is anyone there?' came a whisper.

Nobody replied.

'Charmer? Are you there?' It was Ranger.

'So that's his game,' Fox snarled. 'The traitor! He's led his father to our refuge.'

'Wait, Father,' Charmer pleaded. 'Perhaps he's come to help.'

Before Fox could stop her she had run towards the invader. 'Here I am – it's me, Charmer.'

Fox dashed after his daughter. 'Get outside before I kill you,' he threatened Ranger.

'You don't understand,' Ranger said urgently. 'I ran on ahead of the others. I'll tell them the sett's empty.'

Fox was surprised by these words. Before he could reply, a sneering voice which he immediately recognized, called down the tunnel, 'The game's up, my friend. Your hideout is surrounded. Ranger, come here! We'll fight them in the open when we've starved them out.'

Ranger turned unwillingly. 'At any rate, you have one less to fight,' he whispered to Fox. 'I'll have no part in this.'

The hated Scarface chuckled outside.

'We'll all die,' wailed a fieldmouse.

'No!' cried Fox. 'Not while I'm alive. It's me that scarfaced killer really wants dead. So let him pit himself against me in a fair fight. I'll challenge him to single combat.'

Vixen watched her mate worriedly as he stepped out into the sunlight. Scarface yapped in triumph as he saw Fox emerge. Tawny Owl and Kestrel flew close to lend support.

Fox looked around the enemy throng. 'You've come in strength,' he said to Scarface. 'Do you need all these to overcome me?'

'You're not alone,' Scarface snapped. 'You've plenty of followers.'

83

'Not followers – friends,' Fox corrected him. 'You have no dispute with them. It's me you fear.'

Scarface's eyes blazed. 'Fear?' he bellowed. 'I didn't get these scars through fear! I'm afraid of nothing!'

'Prove it then,' Fox taunted him. 'Dare you fight me?'

'Why, you – ' Scarface spluttered. 'I'll teach you a lesson. And when I've killed you, I'll fight your cubs one by one, and destroy them all.'

Fox said, 'And if I win, my friends are to go un-harmed.'

Scarface grinned cynically. 'All this for a few mice and hedgehogs,' he mocked. 'Very well, you have your wish.'

Fox knew the risk he was taking. Scarface was battle-hardened and experienced. However, on Fox's side were youth and agility.

Fox stood on the defensive. Scarface rushed at him but Fox dropped to his belly. Scarface's attack missed its mark. Ranger and the other onlookers shifted nervously. Now Scarface leapt on Fox, bowling him over and driving the breath from his body. Fox gasped desperately. Scarface drove for his opponent's throat. Fox scrambled clear in the nick of time, gulping down air. Scarface sensed victory. He dashed at Fox, baring his teeth for the kill. He got a grip on Fox's muzzle and tasted blood. Fox kicked out with his forelegs and dislodged Scarface, then bit deeply into the old warrior's chest. Scarface was beaten down as Fox held fast with all his strength.

Scarface fell on his back and Fox aimed for his throat. He had the dominant position now. Scarface began to choke.

Fox was no killer. He meant only to weaken his enemy so much that he would be unwilling to fight ever again. Suddenly Kestrel shrieked, 'The Warden is coming this way!'

Fox held on some moments longer. Scarface's eyes were glazed. Fox released him and ran back into Badger's sett. Scarface lay still, his breath rattling through his gaping jaws. Ranger and his kin scattered as the Warden appeared, then bent to help the injured fox. Scarface made a feeble snap at his hand, then struggled to his feet and limped away.

Fox was greeted as a hero by all his family and Badger, but the smaller animals were less enthusiastic.

'You should have killed him,' Vole complained.

'The Warden came,' Vixen explained.

'Scarface won't be back,' Fox panted wearily. 'And his tribe have lost heart.' Vixen began to lick her mate's wounds.

Weasel said, 'It's a pity, though, you couldn't finish the job. Scarface will still be able to attack small creatures like us.'

Bold said stoutly, 'It'll be a long while before he can do anything dangerous. He's as good as finished.'

But the mice and voles were not convinced that the threat from Scarface was over.

# CHAPTER SEVEN

Adder finally recovered from her mauling, and emerged to eat and sunbathe. She was conscious of her blunted tail and felt neglected. No-one had come to enquire after her. One day, however, she saw Toad splashing happily in the stream and called to him.

'Adder, is that you?' Toad answered. 'Oh, what's happened to your poor tail?'

'A slight disagreement with Scarface,' Adder drawled.

'Scarface again,' Toad croaked. 'When was this?'

'A while back. I've been lying low.'

'Well then, you'll be glad to know there's been a battle since. Fox nearly killed that scarfaced brute.'

Adder leered. 'He's not dead then?'

'No.'

'Good. I have a score to settle with that beast.'

'Please don't risk more injury to yourself,' Toad begged her.

Adder was pleased by his concern. 'Thank you, old friend, for your interest,' she lisped. 'But don't worry. The last scrap was on land, but next time I shall be underwater.'

Toad was completely mystified but Adder refused to reveal her plan.

Scarface was healing. In his case the wounds to his body were less deep than those to his pride. He was unable to hunt and had to rely entirely on his mate's hunting. Meanwhile his son Ranger's friendship with Charmer continued to strengthen. They hunted together, they played together and they knew that they had the approval of Charmer's father and mother. They were able to exchange news from both fox camps. It was certain that neither side wanted to fight again. Only the feelings of Scarface himself were unknown.

'What mood is your father in?' Charmer asked one night.

'Subdued. Quiet. He hates being so helpless. I think he resents it.'

Some distance away Bold watched the fox pair. Despite his father's change of heart, Bold didn't approve of Ranger's close friendship with Charmer. Ranger was still Scarface's cub and Bold remembered how he had been ambushed and imprisoned by Ranger and the others. He greeted the two half-heartedly. 'You're spending a lot of time together,' he remarked.

'Perhaps you should try and mix a little with my family,' Ranger suggested. 'I have some delightful sisters.'

'Is it likely I'd want anything to do with a relative of Scarface?' Bold retorted.

'Can't you forget my father?' Ranger pleaded. 'We're not all like him. Things are different now.'

'We shall see,' said Bold. 'If I know Scarface he'll be biding his time until he's ready to strike again. Many of my father's old friends think he should have killed Scarface when he had the chance.'

Bold's words proved true. As soon as Scarface felt strong enough, he set off alone to get his revenge. He hunted the more defenceless Farthing Wood creatures, slaughtering fieldmice and almost all the voles. Scarface wolfed down their tiny bodies. Then he went further. Four young rabbits and a squirrel were savaged. Since Fox's triumph over the hateful animal, the night watches had ceased and so, when news reached Fox, he blamed himself.

'They were right, the little creatures,' he moaned. 'I should have finished him!'

'The Warden – ' Vixen began.

'No. I could have done it,' Fox interrupted. 'And now, look how they've all suffered, because of me.'

'You weren't to know, you weren't to know,' Vixen tried to console him.

'I can't bring them back,' Fox groaned, 'but I can make amends. I can still save those who are left.' He prepared to go at once and confront the sly slayer. As he loped sorrowfully away he didn't know that the task he had just set himself had already been carried out by another.

Scarface had been seen by Adder on the night he had crept away alone on his mission of murder. There was something about the beast's air as he swam the stream that made Adder decide he was up to no good. 'He'll come back this way,' she hissed to herself, 'and he won't be expecting to meet *me*.'

Under cover of darkness she slithered into the water and anchored herself to a thick growth of weed. Now she had only to wait for the cruel fox's return.

By the dawn light she saw him approach. He sat down on the bank and yawned. His expression was crafty and self-satisfied. At last Scarface waded into the stream and began to swim back across. Adder untangled herself and slid into the stream, too. Then, with just her head above water, she wriggled close. Striking from beneath the fox she sank her poisonous fangs deep into Scarface's soft belly. Scarface yelped with pain and kicked out for the far bank. Adder allowed herself to float downstream on the current.

Her victim dragged himself on to dry land. He knew only too well what had happened. 'I'm done for,' he muttered. 'Farthing Wood has taken its revenge.' He thought of the animals he had just killed and was somehow comforted by those deeds. Presently Adder came to enjoy her moment of triumph. Scarface spotted her blunt tail.

'So it was you,' he gasped. 'I've – paid – for not – catching you when I should.'

'You've got your just reward,' Adder leered.

Scarface shuddered. 'You've killed – me,' he panted, 'but remember. You'll never – rid yourself – of my mark.' He keeled over and lay still.

While Adder and her news were welcomed as never before by the remaining Farthing Wood animals, the discovery of Scarface's carcass by his relatives produced a mixture of reactions. Few, except his mate, mourned his passing. There was little love lost between their leader and Scarface's tribe. Amongst these, Ranger realized, a new age was dawning in White Deer Park. There was now no obstacle in the path of his and Charmer's friendship. And there was no reason why Charmer's brothers shouldn't form closer ties with the young foxes on Ranger's side. A more peaceful time lay ahead for everyone.

'We can start to think about the best site for our den,' Charmer said to Ranger. 'We have the whole of the Park to choose from now.'

'Yes, there's a new feeling of freedom amongst all of us,' he replied. 'For me, home is where the heart is. And wherever you are, Charmer, there my heart follows.'

Friendly and Bold, too, were keen to roam further afield. 'Shall we take a look around the rest of the Reserve?' Friendly suggested.

'Why stop there?' Bold shrugged. 'There's a whole world outside White Deer Park.'

'But – it's dangerous out there!' Friendly exclaimed.

Bold laughed. 'It hasn't been exactly safe inside here recently. And why should I confine myself to one small area? I'm going to make full use of our new freedom.'

The brother cubs looked at each other. They both knew they had to separate.

'Well . . .' Bold began.

'Go carefully,' said Friendly.

'You too,' Bold answered. 'And good luck.'

Fox and Vixen, together with their friends, were congratulating Adder. 'Not for the first time you are a heroine,' Vixen said. 'I shall always remember how you saved me from certain death on our journey here.'

Adder's tongue flickered. 'A pleasure, Vixen. But you can be sure, while I nursed my wound, I nursed a desire for revenge too. When the time came – '

'Oh Adder,' Fox broke in. 'How ashamed I am of our neglect. Until Toad brought the news, none of us knew about your injury. Please don't stray so far from your friends in the future. And, as for us, well – we'd like to keep you company now and then.'

Adder leered. 'Obliged, I'm sure,' she hissed. 'But do you speak for all?'

Badger and Weasel, Owl and Mole hastily affirmed their friendship. 'Nothing can separate the Farthing Wood animals,' said Badger. 'We've been through too much together.'

While he spoke, Bold was squeezing through the Park boundary fence. He paused, sniffing the air, on the threshold of a new world. New scents, new sounds, sent a thrill of adventure through his young body. He ran on into open country in the gathering dusk.

Part III

# THE FOX CUB BOLD

# CHAPTER ONE

Bold ran alone on the downland. At daybreak he paused to look around him. The landscape was quiet and seemingly empty, except for a bird or two. 'This is the real world,' the young fox said to himself with satisfaction, 'the wild, natural world.' He ran across the turf, swift and confident.

A solitary crow on a tree-top watched him pass. 'Well, well,' it muttered. 'A fox abroad in the day-time. *He'll* learn the hard way.'

Bold was hungry. A dead pigeon attracted both his and the crow's attention. The bird flew down to peck at the carrion. Bold chased away the crow and tore off some mouthfuls. The angry crow scolded him.

'Most foxes *I* know hunt their prey by night,' it chattered. 'They don't need to steal others' food in the daytime.'

Bold looked up. 'I never ignore the chance of a bite,' he replied. 'But, rest assured, I know all about night hunting. Here – you're welcome to this heap of feathers. I'll get something tastier.' He left the pigeon for the crow.

'You'll get something more than just tasty if you

stay around here in full view,' the bird called after him. 'I don't know where you came from, but the foxes in these parts are far more wily than you. And they need to be!'

Bold laughed. 'I'm in search of adventure,' he cried.

The crow screeched back, 'Well, I think you'll find it!'

By the end of that first day, Bold had travelled a long way. He rested under a hawthorn tree whose boughs bent over a stream. Already White Deer Park, his family and friends were out of his mind. A large bird landed in the crown of the hawthorn. Bold glanced up. It was the crow again!

'Oh-ho,' it croaked. 'Here's the bold young fox.'

'That's my name,' said Bold. 'Bold by nature.'

'So I've seen,' the crow replied. 'Let me give you some advice. You should curb your boldness before it gets you into trouble.'

'Thank you for your warning,' Bold answered sarcastically, 'but really I've nothing to fear. And now, if you don't mind, I'd like to sleep.'

Over the next few weeks Bold ranged far and wide. He entered an area of farmland and scattered houses. Bold was confident he would survive on his own: he had eaten well and regularly, he was a skilful hunter and he had grown into a fine fox – well-built, swift-footed and tireless. He felt that he was a match for anyone.

There was plenty of food of all types. Once he killed a partridge as it rose from the ground in front of him, and from then on he had a taste for game birds. One evening he came to a place where the scent of game was very strong. It was a wooded area enclosed by a rickety fence which was no obstacle to a fox as determined as Bold.

Inside the wood where the ground was soft Bold found footprints – human prints – and the smell of humans was in the air. But he cared nothing for that. He was on the trail of something of greater interest. His mouth watered as he stole through the under-growth.

He scared a hen pheasant out of some brambles and felled her with a quick bite. Then he looked around for somewhere safe to eat his catch. Under the roots of a beech he found a badger's sett. The owner was absent and, since Bold was used to the Farthing Wood Badger and thought of all his kind as friendly, he went inside, made himself comfortable and feasted off his kill.

Towards morning the sett's owner returned. Bold sensed the badger's presence and prepared to leave. A female badger was hesitating at the entrance, having caught Bold's smell.

'Don't be alarmed,' said Bold. 'I'm leaving.'

'Foxes and badgers keep apart in this wood,' she replied. 'I haven't seen you before.'

'I'm a stranger to the area,' Bold told her. 'I came here by chance.'

'The same chance that brings many foxes here – game. But most don't stay for long.'

'Because of competition?' Bold asked.

'Not the sort you're thinking of,' the badger answered.

'What then?'

'Haven't you seen the footprints?'

'Oh *those*. They don't bother me,' Bold answered carelessly.

'Well, they should. Humans are your real competitors for game. This wood is full of game birds, because humans raise them and release them here. And if you knew humans, you'd know they don't like interference in their plans. There's one human around here always with an eye open for animals like you who are after his precious birds. So – beware!'

'Another warning!' Bold laughed. 'Yet you live here without trouble, it seems. So I'll take *my* chances.'

Bold left the wood at daylight and kept his distance until dusk fell. Then he returned and another pheasant fell victim to the young fox.

Night after night the same pattern was repeated. Bold's stealth kept him clear of the gamekeeper, but both were aware of the other's presence. From time to time he saw the badger sow who never repeated her warning, but only showed surprise at Bold's nerve.

'He'll never catch *me*,' Bold boasted. 'My skill will see to that.'

# CHAPTER TWO

One night as Bold hunted he heard a sharp cry of pain, followed by the most piteous squeals and snorts. He hurried towards the sound. He found the sow badger caught fast in a horrible metal trap. Her struggles were useless and only tightened the trap's vice-like grip. Bold was horrified by the animal's obvious agony. Ruefully he realized the trap had almost certainly been set for him. But it was the poor badger who had blundered into it.

'I'll try to help you,' Bold said.

The badger, now still, cowered in severe pain. She was astonished by the young fox's offer, knowing nothing of Bold's upbringing under the Farthing Wood Oath.

There was a strong wire which looped over the badger's back and pinned her body to the ground. Bold saw that, from outside the trap, the end of this wire might be snapped by strong jaws. He bit at it. The badger winced.

'I'm sorry,' said Bold. 'This may take a long time.' He paused, listening and watching for sound or sight of the gamekeeper. Nothing. Bold's teeth got to work again, rasping at the metal. Many minutes passed. And then he heard it – the tramp of human footsteps. He bit and gnawed desperately, knowing that in a few minutes he must flee. The weakened wire suddenly snapped with a fierce backward lash that nearly blinded him. The badger wriggled free and dashed for her sett. Bold raced after her.

Inside the sett, the two animals gasped for breath. Bold's eye streamed with water and, in the corner, blood ran from the gash made by the point of the wire. The badger's back bled where the loop of the trap had punctured her hide. They licked each other's sores. Then, tired out by their ordeal, they both fell asleep.

The badger sow awoke first, still amazed by her escape and how the fox had freed her. She stood over her saviour. Her breath woke him. Bold's good eye opened. The injured one remained closed.

'I can never thank you enough,' the badger murmured.

'The trap was meant for me,' Bold answered. 'How could I let you suffer in my place?'

'But you have wounded yourself for my sake.'

'Wounds heal,' said Bold. 'Think nothing of it. And tomorrow I move on. I see now I shouldn't risk staying here.'

'Wisely spoken,' the badger agreed. 'And now you have a friend. If ever you need help, remember me.'

'Thank you. I shall,' Bold replied.

Within the area of farmland, but away from the

game wood, was a dense thicket of gorse. This was ideal for Bold to lie in during the day, and it became his regular refuge. One morning he awoke with a start to the sound of gunfire. His injured eye watered a good deal. Bold rubbed at it impatiently with a paw and raised himself to peer through the spiky stems.

He saw a line of men standing at intervals along the crest of a ridge. All were carrying guns. Beaters sent waves of pheasant or partridge scrambling from the undergrowth into the sky. There the birds' panicky flight took them into the men's line of fire. Birds crumpled and plummeted to earth where large dogs ran to fetch them. Bold's heart pounded and he quivered every time a gun was fired. Should he run or stay under cover?

Suddenly a pheasant crashed lifeless to the ground only a short distance away. Bold saw a retriever bounding towards it. The fox's mind was made up. He dashed away from the gorse patch. His poor eye flooded with water from the cold of the autumn air. He seemed to be running in a mist and so didn't realize the danger. There was a second line of guns and he was racing towards it! One of the men had just taken a reloaded gun. He saw the fox clearly and, seeing no birds, turned his fire on Bold. Bold veered away but heard the sharp crack of the gun. Instantly he felt a fierce pain searing his right thigh. He fell.

Bold was at the mercy of the men and the dogs. He waited for the end. But at that moment partridges fluttered overhead and the guns were once more turned on them.

Bold hauled himself up. His wounded leg could bear no weight at all and, as he tried to stand on it, a fresh surge of pain ran through it. Bold knew his luck wouldn't last and he had to get away. He forced himself to move on his three sound legs and limped slowly, dragging his useless leg along the ground. The field took an age to cross. Every second he expected to be shot down, but somehow he managed to reach a drainage ditch into which he collapsed and was hidden from view.

His wound throbbed agonizingly. Some water in the ditch cooled his body a little and he lapped at the moisture. He turned to lick at his wounded thigh. There was a clean hole in it. The lead shot had passed right through, but had torn the muscle badly. Bold's body seemed to be filled with the relentless throb of pain.

He looked along the ditch. Ahead there was better cover where it ran through a spinney. He dragged himself along until some overhanging branches gave him better shelter. Still the noise of gunfire rang in the air. Bold laid his head on his paws. Whatever happened now he could move no farther. He was exhausted.

Bold slept. It was quite dark when he awoke again. Everything was quiet. No guns, no dogs, no men. He heaved a sigh. He was very thirsty. Thirst was no problem but how was he to feed himself? His bad leg had stiffened during the night and his fur was caked with blood around the wound. He tried to raise himself but sank back at once, unable even to bend his injured limb. Bold realized he was a cripple.

He felt very alone. The fox who had craved independence and freedom now longed for company. How things had changed! He tried to move again. Gritting his teeth, he hauled himself on to his three good legs and pulled himself into the wood. He hobbled forward. He was very hungry. He was bitter to think that he was was now incapable of hunting. He would have to eat food such as worms and insects. A bramble bush laden with blackberries attracted his attention. Fruit was a good stand-by too.

As Bold snapped off the ripest berries, he spotted a dormouse who was feasting off the fruit too. The little creature sat on its haunches on a twig as it munched at a big berry held in its paws. Here was a welcome addition to Bold's meal if he could only catch it. He froze. The dormouse crept closer and closer as it sought its food. Bold was too eager and too desperate. He lunged forward but his jaws closed on thin air. The dormouse leapt to the ground in fright and scuttled away. Bold knew it was useless to give chase.

'You're lucky I'm injured,' Bold growled at the dormouse who had escaped into another bush and now watched him limping.

'If you can't even catch a mouse, you'll soon starve to death,' it squeaked at him.

'Just you wait!' Bold barked. 'When my leg's mended things will be different.'

'I won't hold my breath,' the dormouse mocked him.

Bold was humiliated. To be scoffed at by a mouse! He turned back to the berries, feeling sick at heart. All his pride and self-confidence vanished. Later he crept under some shrubbery to nurse his wound and his misery.

## CHAPTER THREE

For a week or two Bold remained in the spinney. Rain brought worms, slugs and snails into the open. This was his daily diet, occasionally enriched by a rare find of carrion. He moved around very little. His leg hurt him less but he knew now it was damaged for ever. He couldn't stretch or bend it. He would never be able to run or leap again as he had once loved to do. The best he could manage was a kind of uneven lurch.

As temperatures dropped and frost nipped the air, even snails and slugs became scarce. Bold was soon famished – thin and weak. The smaller animals in the spinney had long ago discovered this fox was not to be feared. They ran around him regardless, and even competed for the poor scraps Bold relied upon. Bold's will to live wavered. What point was there in struggling to survive? He was no longer a fox in the true sense of the word, but a pitiful scrounging creature: an invalid. Yet he never thought of returning to White Deer Park. Even had he believed he could reach it, his last shred of pride prevented it. He had made his choice by leaving the Reserve. There was no going back.

Then one day he remembered the badger sow's promise to help him. Perhaps she could bring him some proper food. With properly nourishing food he would maybe revive sufficiently to see the winter through. His spirits rose just a little and he set out for the game wood.

But Bold had left it too late. He was too weak now for any kind of travelling, and he soon realized he could never cover the distance. He sank down in the drainage ditch, his breath coming in gasps, his poor wasted body shuddering with the undue effort. This was it then. This was where he would die.

A solitary black bird circled overhead, waiting for the animal's last breath. Bold lay still. The bird flew down and hopped close to check on him.

Bold watched it with his good eye. 'You'll have . . . to wait . . . a little longer,' he panted.

The bird gave a croak of surprise. 'Not the bold young fox?' it cried.

Bold recognized the crow of his first days of freedom. 'So it's you? Well, you did warn me . . .'

'What's happened to you?'

'My leg's injured. I was shot. Can't walk.'

'So you're starving?'

'I am,' Bold admitted. 'I was too weak . . . to fetch help. Now I've no-one to call on.'

The crow put his head on one side. 'Who would help you?'

'A badger. One I rescued from a trap.'

'Where is this badger? Why doesn't it come?'

'She doesn't know . . . I need her,' Bold muttered.

106

He looked steadily at the crow. 'If only I had . . . a messenger . . .'

The crow looked steadily back. 'You don't think . . . ? No, no, what an idea! Why should I?'

'*You* can *fly*,' Bold sighed. 'How long would it take you? Would you have . . . my death on your conscience?'

'Conscience?' the crow cried. 'Why my conscience? Your pride brought you to this pass. That's all.'

Bold's head sank back. 'Then the cub of the Farthing Wood Fox . . . will die through lack . . . of a friend.'

The crow looked at him sharply. '*You*? His offspring? So that's it! You came from the Nature Reserve. You left a safe haven for – for – pride's sake!'

'I admit it. Now, will you help?'

'I'll try,' the crow said in a completely different tone. 'The Farthing Wood Fox's cub – well well! Where is the badger?'

Bold explained. The crow took to the air and Bold was left to his thoughts. 'So, Father,' he murmured. 'Even here I'm dependent on your name.'

A moment later the crow returned. 'Here,' it croaked, dropping a hunk of meat. 'I tore this off a rabbit carcass. It'll keep you going for a while.'

Bold gulped it down. 'You're very kind,' he gasped.

'Think nothing of it. Want some more?'

Bold's look was sufficient answer. The bird

wheeled away. When it returned it carried a much larger chunk of the dead animal.

'There! Now I'm on my way.'

The food put new heart into Bold and he waited eagerly for his friend the badger to arrive.

It was a long journey from the game wood. The female badger carried as much food as she could. She brought with her three male cubs, now grown up, from her last litter, who carried extra supplies. The animals travelled cautiously in the daylight, guided by the crow. They found Bold in the ditch. They dropped the food – tubers, bulbs, a large rat, mice – and watched him eat without a word.

Bold devoured it all, piece by piece. At last his friend spoke. 'I barely recognize you.'

'Fortune turned against me,' Bold said bluntly.

'We heard your story from the crow,' said the badger mother. 'I'm sorry to see you like this. Perhaps you should have stayed in the game wood?'

'Perhaps I should,' Bold grunted. 'I could hardly have done worse.'

'Well, you must build up your strength. It's almost dusk. We'll see if we can find you something more in the spinney.'

'Huh! There's no rich harvest in there,' Bold remarked sourly. 'I've been trying to live off it for a long while.'

'We'll do our best,' said the badger.

'Of course. I didn't mean . . . I'm most grateful to you all. Really I am,' Bold replied quickly.

'I know. Don't fret,' the badger answered. 'Come on, youngsters.'

Bold did feel stronger and, after another lot of food, he was ready to move. 'You must get back,' he told the badgers. 'You'll be exposed here in the daylight with no refuge. Please use the darkness to get home. I'll follow you – at my own pace.'

They looked at him doubtfully but there didn't seem to be an alternative, so they left.

Bold was alone again. He felt refreshed. The pain in his bad leg had almost disappeared. He was able to walk on his three good legs in his own style without too much difficulty. The injury to his eye had healed but he was aware that his sight was permanently damaged. He set himself to travel a little at a time, taking frequent rests. He headed for the farmland again.

The first field was enclosed by hedgerow. Here he had a piece of luck. He discovered an empty foxes' earth where scraps of food from their kills littered the den. Bold's new appetite made short work of these. Also, he was pretty sure the place had not been used for some time. The scent of fox was faint.

'I can use this,' he said to himself. 'It can be my base. And, meanwhile, I'll explore the area. There must be food somewhere on humans' land.'

There *was* food. Root vegetables and such like – but no meat. And meat was what Bold needed most to stand a real chance of making it through the winter.

One foggy day the injured fox was astounded to

see a large black bird dropping down from a height, its beak stuffed with carrion. The crow placed the meat in front of him. 'You'll be needing this,' the bird said.

'Crow!'

'I've been keeping an eye on you. You don't look too sturdy.'

Bold snatched up the meat. 'This is good,' he mumbled with his mouth full. 'Where did you find it?'

'Oh! There's plenty more of that if you know where to look,' the crow cawed.

'And where's that?'

'In the town.'

'Town?' Bold repeated.

'Yes. Not far from here. Full of humans and their nests. *And* their food.'

'How long would it take me to get there?' Bold demanded eagerly.

'Hard to tell, in your condition,' the crow answered, 'but there's lots of cover on the way.'

'I like the idea of stealing from humans,' Bold growled. 'They made me like this! I'll pay them back for it.'

'That's the spirit. I stole that meat from a dog's food-bowl. We all have to eat.'

'I shall call you Robber,' Bold declared. 'We're friends now. I owe my life to you and the badgers.'

The crow seemed to like his name. 'Robber. Yes, that suits. You and I – we can be a team. We'll look out for each other. When will you start?'

'Tonight,' Bold said determinedly. 'What direction do I take?'

'Watch me,' said Robber. He took to the air and Bold followed his flight. The bird disappeared but Bold had all the information he needed.

# CHAPTER FOUR

When darkness came Bold set his course, following the direction of Robber's flight. He travelled at an easy pace. A faint gleam on the horizon grew steadily brighter as, with each night, he neared the lights of the town.

By the end of the second night, he was on the town's edge. He found some pickings in a litter basket and rested underneath a privet hedge. By dawn the sounds of traffic reached his ears. The noise increased as day broadened. Robber hadn't prepared the fox for this din.

Bold was uneasy. He raised himself and limped about uncertainly. There didn't seem to be any escape, neither was there anywhere to hide from the awful noise. At last a familiar croak brought Robber to his side.

'Follow me,' said the bird. He led Bold to a patch of waste ground. Here there was bramble, thick brown weeds and shrubs. 'You'll be safe here,' said Robber.

'I shall never get used to that racket,' Bold complained. 'Whatever is it? Is it humans?'

'Sort of. Humans' machines. And you'll *have* to

get used to it, if you're going to remain here. Besides, you'll be scavenging by night. It's much quieter then.'

'I hope so,' Bold muttered.

'Now,' said Robber. 'Remember. Team-work. You'll be able to reach food that I can't. And I'll be about in the daytime. So, between us, we can work this patch for all it's worth.'

'I'll share everything I find with you,' Bold promised. 'I owe you a lot.'

'Good. I'll rustle something up now. You stay put.'

Bold hid himself and was soon fast asleep. Robber returned and cawed the fox awake. Bold found a packet of sandwiches in front of his nose.

'What's this?' he asked suspiciously.

'Human food,' Robber answered. 'I've eaten what I want.'

Bold sniffed at it. 'It smells all right,' he acknowledged. He had never seen bread before. He clawed at the paper and took a bite of bread and cheese.

'You have to accept what comes,' Robber told him. 'You can't overlook anything.'

'This is good,' Bold remarked gratefully. 'And tonight, it'll be my turn.'

Robber had been right. By evening the town was quieter. Bold went limping across the fields, smelling many new scents. He came to a group of buildings. They were in darkness. Walls or fences surrounded them and their plots of land. Bold realized at once that, since he could no longer jump, these areas were closed to him unless he could slip through a gap or scramble underneath the barriers.

He did succeed in visiting several gardens and yards. And here he discovered dustbins! The wealth and variety of food scraps these contained was remarkable.

'I shall never go hungry,' Bold told himself. 'What a find!' He actually began to feel cheerful. He became quite absorbed in his explorations. He snapped up pieces of stale bread left for the birds. And in one garden he found two food-bowls, one with milk in it, the other meat. He swallowed the contents gratefully.

Bold learnt to hide himself briefly if a dustbin made a crash. Sometimes a clatter did bring a human outside to investigate, but there was usually a bush or shrub to hide in. If not, he got himself out of the garden and well away before he could be noticed. He carried a meaty-looking bone back to the waste-plot for Robber to pick at. It was dawn when he got back and Bold was completely tired out.

'This is welcome,' Robber greeted him. The crow pecked vigorously at the fragments of meat. Bold burrowed into the vegetation to sleep.

The next night Bold combed a different area and now he found there were competitors for this food supply. Sleet was falling and, as Bold peered into a large garden, he saw through the downpour another fox – a brisk, confident-looking animal – trotting purposefully across the lawn. Bold tensed. The fox went straight to a stone bird-table and, quite effort-lessly, leapt up to the flat top. The grace and ease of the fox, which Bold knew to be female, impressed him tremendously. At the same time this was a bit-ter reminder of how he had once been. Now, by comparison, what a poor physical specimen he must appear! His brush drooped and he turned to slink away.

As if to underline his sad state, the vixen came straight towards him, lithe and agile. She leapt the fence athletically, landing a metre or so from Bold. She saw him but showed no curiosity. For a moment the two foxes stared at each other; then the vixen trotted coolly away.

Bold was humiliated by her lack of interest. Only too aware of his changed appearance, this was a further blow to his self-esteem. If only she had seen him as he once was! Bold crawled homeward, feel-ing thoroughly hopeless.

The next day Robber left Bold some food fragments as usual. Later he noticed his friend hadn't emerged from his sleeping quarters. He flew down and found Bold, lying miserably on his side.

'Not hungry?' Robber croaked.

'*You* eat it,' Bold murmured.

'Feeling sorry for yourself?'

'Wouldn't you, if you looked like me?'

'Oh, you'll soon fatten up with regular food,' Robber cried. 'At least you're still alive. You might have died in that ditch!'

'I know. I don't mean to be ungrateful,' muttered

Bold. 'But, you see, I'll never run or jump again. So what's the good of it all? And my own kind ignore me.'

'Oh-ho. So that's it!' Robber eclaimed. 'You've seen another fox?'

'Yes. A vixen.'

'Well, that's good then. Try and make friends. Don't be so down-hearted.'

'Look at me,' Bold moaned. 'Why should she even give me a glance?'

'Well, if you don't eat when you can, you'll never improve your appearance,' Robber declared. 'Come on, I brought this specially.'

Bold stirred himself and obediently gulped down the scraps. Robber had managed to cheer him a little. 'Thank you,' he said. 'I'm glad to have you as my friend anyway.'

## CHAPTER FIVE

For several nights, Bold looked for the vixen. He stared through the fence into the large garden with the bird-table, but never caught a glimpse of her there. Then one evening, there she was. Bold longed to join her but the wooden fence was between them. Well, he couldn't jump, but he could dig!

He began to scrape at the soil. It was soft. Bold dug harder. The hole went deeper and deeper, but somehow he couldn't seem to get down to the base of the fence. He looked up to check on the vixen's presence. She had gone! Suddenly she landed with a muffled thud beside him, having leapt over the top again.

'Can't you jump?' she asked.

Bold started, then muttered, 'No,' trying to tuck his damaged leg under his body.

'You're hurt, aren't you?'

'I – I was injured. A long time ago,' Bold answered in a low voice.

'You're unfortunate,' the vixen said. 'But you can save yourself any more trouble. There's nothing much of interest in there.'

'No, there isn't now,' Bold agreed in a not very bold voice.

'You were trying to get to *me*,' the vixen said. She looked at Bold curiously. 'I haven't seen you before.'

Bold didn't contradict her. 'I came here from the country. Food was scarce.'

'Hm. Hunting must be difficult for you.'

'What do you mean?' Bold growled, but he knew only too well.

'Why, if you can't jump, you can't run, I suppose.'

'No, I can't,' he snapped. 'And neither could you, if you'd been shot in the leg.'

'My, you're touchy,' the vixen remarked. 'Accidents happen. Tell me about it.'

Bold did so.

'Bad luck indeed,' the vixen said afterwards with sympathy. 'I'm sorry.'

Bold pulled himself out of the hole he had dug. When he tottered forward the vixen realized just how handicapped he was. She softened further. 'If you'd accept help, I'd be glad to give it,' she offered. '*I* could be your legs.'

'I'm not quite helpless!' Bold said.

'Of course not,' she agreed, aware she had touched him on a raw spot. 'Well, goodbye then. And good luck!'

Bold watched her go. He almost called her back, but couldn't quite find his voice. He collected a titbit for Robber and set off home. His own appetite was lost.

The foxes' paths didn't cross again until midwinter. Bold was limping over some playing-fields. The severe cold increased the stiffness of his old wound and, because of the lack of really fresh meat in his diet, he was thinner than ever. The vixen saw him from a distance. She herself was finding the going more tough but, at the sight of Bold, her heart melted. She was filled with compassion and ran after him.

'We meet again,' she said simply, drawing alongside.

Bold glanced at her in astonishment. 'Well,' he said. 'How are things with you?'

'Rather better than with you, probably,' she replied. 'Look, I'd like to help. Why don't we hunt together?'

Bold was delighted. However, he realized who would really do the hunting. 'I'd be glad of your company,' he said.

'Listen then. There's a colony of rats living on an island in the canal. It's quite a way from here. How do you feel about it?'

Bold didn't hesitate. 'Lead on,' he said.

She took him at his own pace to a canal bank. 'See? The water's risen, so they can only escape by swimming. I'll swim out into the canal and catch some. You can snap up any that try to escape.'

The rats panicked as the vixen paddled through the icy water. They squealed and squeaked in terror. Some dived into the water and swam for the shore. Bold was ready for these as they landed. The vixen snapped at the others in the water, killing many. She paddled back, bringing her victims.

'You're a good hunter. And light as a whisper,' Bold complimented her. 'And so I shall call you.'

'Whisper? Then I must have a name for you.'

'I'm called Bold,' he said, 'and bold I once was.'

'And perhaps so again,' Whisper remarked, seeing the pile of rats he had slain. 'You've done well. We've more than enough here. Well, Bold – let's eat.'

They took as much as they wanted and hid the rest of their catch under a pile of soil and twigs, intending to return for them the next day. Bold picked up one carcass to carry back for Robber.

'Are you still hungry?' Whisper asked.

Bold shook his head. He dropped the rat. 'It's for an old partner – a crow. He brings me food and I him. He saved my life once.'

Whisper said, 'Perhaps you won't be needing this partner any more? It's for you to decide.'

Bold said nothing for the moment.

'Well, I'll be at the waterside tomorrow night,' said the vixen.

'And so will I,' Bold replied.

Robber was delighted to see fresh food. 'A rat! So you're a hunter again.'

'I had help,' Bold explained.

'Oh? Not the – '

'Yes. The vixen. We've become friends.'

'Good. Then our arrangement is at an end?' Robber asked.

'Will you be all right?' Bold asked.

'Of course,' the crow said.

'Well,' said Bold. 'If you do need me, or you want to see me, leave something as a message under the hedge there, by the playing fields. And I'll do the same.'

'All right,' said Robber. 'I understand. I hope we won't become complete strangers?'

'No fear of that,' said Bold.

The next night Bold and Whisper uncovered their store of food by the canal and ate together.

'Do you have a den?' Whisper asked.

'Not a proper one,' Bold answered. 'I sleep above ground.'

'You can share my earth,' Whisper offered, 'if you wish. Unless your other ties . . .'

'I have no other ties,' Bold said.

After they had finished their meal Whisper led her new companion along different paths to the other side of the town. Her earth was on the far side of the churchyard, under a large overhanging tree. There was a mat of ivy underfoot.

'It's well concealed,' Bold commented as he followed Whisper inside. 'And warm too.'

'Are you tired?' she asked him.

'Yes. But content.'

'I'm glad. I think you've found life very hard recently?'

Bold nodded.

'You must have seen several winters already?' Whisper murmured.

121

'No, no.' Bold shook his head. 'I've yet to survive my first winter.'

Whisper's mouth dropped open. 'Your *first*? But . . . but . . . it can't be true!'

'It's certainly true,' Bold assured her irritably. 'I was born last spring.'

'I'm sorry. I thought . . . of course, your injury . . .' Whisper was embarrassed.

'I hadn't realized I'd aged so much,' Bold muttered bitterly.

'You've suffered a great deal,' Whisper said with sympathy. 'I'm actually a season older than you. Were you born nearby?'

'No – a long way away. I roamed widely before my injury. I was born in a Nature Reserve. A place called White Deer Park.'

'Why ever did you leave such a safe place?' Whisper asked in amazement.

'My own curiosity. And pride. I wanted to live in what I thought was the Real World. To meet its dangers. To be independent. Of course, I've paid for my stupidity. I shall never be strong and healthy and *free* any more.'

'Free from what?'

'My father's influence.'

'Your father?'

'Yes,' Bold answered. 'The famous Farthing Wood Fox. I always felt under his shadow.'

'You – the cub of the Farthing Wood Fox?' Whisper drew a sharp breath.

Her reaction was expected. Bold was becoming used to this.

'You've been foolish, Bold,' Whisper said, 'but how brave too!' She gazed at him in admiration and an idea began to form in her mind.

As for Bold, his head was full of thoughts. Of his old home, his family, his mother Vixen – more graceful, more lithe even than Whisper. Did she think of him? He was sure she did. But he was also sure she would never see her bold, brave young cub again . . .

## CHAPTER SIX

Whisper had decided to make it her task to bring Bold back to health, and she told him so.

'You're very kind,' he told her gratefully. 'But my leg will never mend.'

'I'll see you have flesh on your bones anyway,' Whisper answered with determination.

Bold sighed. 'I'm so glad I met you,' he said.

'Mine was the luck,' she replied gently, but she didn't explain why for the moment.

Bold soon noticed, however, that she was true to her word. Whatever they found or caught to eat, Whisper made sure he had the best of it. Sometimes they were lucky and ate well; at other times they only scraped by. But Bold did gain weight.

'I'm quite pleased with you,' Whisper said one day. 'You're certainly a little plumper.'

'Well, I do feel a little stronger,' Bold remarked. 'And some of my old confidence is coming back, Whisper. It's all due to you.'

'I'm so glad,' she murmured. 'We shall need it.'

Bold felt now he had a new purpose in life. He looked forward to the end of winter when he and Whisper could leave the town and return to open

124

country. His step was less laboured, his bad eye was forgotten. And in his new jaunty mood he decided to look for his old friend Robber. He left a message under the hedge in the shape of a titbit, hoping the crow would find it.

Early next morning Robber found the scrap. He knew at once Bold had been by, and set off in search of him. Bold was keeping a look-out for him from the churchyard.

'Bold!' Robber screeched as he detected the fox. 'You wanted me?'

'Just to know how you're making out?'

'I appreciate that,' Robber croaked, landing beside him. 'My, *you've* improved. Your new life agrees with you – that's obvious.'

'And you?'

'Oh, can't complain. I'll survive.' Robber chuckled. 'Perhaps I'll find myself a mate like you and get fat!'

The new year came. The winter weather had not been too severe. Whisper knew she was carrying Bold's cubs and decided on a plan. As she and Bold lay comfortably in their den, Whisper said, 'Very soon we must leave here.'

'Soon?' Bold queried. 'Why return to the country before the winter's over?'

'Our journey *must* be made before the end of winter,' Whisper answered. 'It's a long one and we need a safe place for our cubs to be born in.'

'Surely it's safe enough here?' Bold suggested. 'And what's this talk of a journey?' He was puzzled.

'I want our cubs to be born in the Nature Reserve as you were.'

Bold gasped. 'White Deer Park?' he whispered.

'Certainly. You must take us there.'

Bold saw the sense in the plan but felt sick at heart. 'I – I never thought of returning there,' he muttered. 'Tell me truthfully, Whisper. Is this why you chose me for your mate? I often wondered why you did. There are plenty of stronger, healthier males around.'

'Yes, I always thought your knowledge of the Nature Reserve would be an advantage,' Whisper admitted. 'But it was your father that impressed me, too.'

Bold's head sank. 'My father again! Am I never to be recognized for myself?'

'Of course you are,' Whisper assured him hastily. 'You are a brave, courageous animal. And that is because of the Farthing Wood blood in your veins. I'm proud of you.'

'So now I must abandon the life I chose,' Bold commented bitterly, 'to creep back with my tail between my legs?'

'It's for the sake of your cubs,' Whisper reminded him.

Bold knew there could be no argument with that. 'Yes, yes,' he nodded wearily. 'I'll take you there. Never fear.'

Whisper was eager to begin the journey. She made Bold eat extra food, taking less herself, over the next

126

few days. She wanted to be as sure as she could that he was fit enough to travel.

The day came when Whisper felt Bold must be ready. He looked stouter than at any time since she had first met him. 'I think we should leave,' she told him simply. 'Tonight.'

Bold just had time to leave a message for Robber. He wasn't going to leave his old friend out of their plans. Some time later the crow found the titbit and flew to the foxes' earth. He perched on a yew branch and called for Bold. Bold heard the familiar croaks.

'Robber, I'm glad you came,' he said. 'Whisper and I leave here tonight. We're travelling a long way – all the way to my birthplace. Our cubs are to be born there.'

'Oh, so cubs are due, are they?' Robber cawed. 'That's good news. Are you sure you're up to this journey?'

'It's Whisper's idea,' Bold explained. 'I have my doubts. It's a formidable distance for a three-legged fox.'

Robber put his head on one side. 'It makes sense for the cubs but . . .' He didn't finish. 'Look,' he interrupted himself, 'I'll keep you in sight as you go. Then, if you ever need help again . . .'

'Thank you, Robber. I was hoping you'd say something like that.'

The pair of foxes began their trek that night. Whisper wisely allowed Bold to set the pace. They travelled steadily and noiselessly. By dawn they had put the town well behind them and were into open country. They entered a patch of woodland to rest. Huddling together for warmth, they were soon asleep. Robber found their slumbering bodies and vanished again. The countryside had once more become his territory too.

The next night the foxes' first need was to find food. Whisper had to do the hunting as usual. Bold was thankful not to have this burden. After eating, they continued on. And this was the pattern of their journey. Their travelling time was ruled by the need to eat and so was limited. This suited Bold perfectly, for it didn't put too much of a strain on his bad leg.

Eventually, however, Whisper fretted. 'We must try to speed up a bit, Bold,' she urged. 'We've come such a little way.'

'We're doing all right,' he answered, knowing better than she did about the distance to White Deer Park. 'We have to eat.'

By the first week of February they had reached an area of farmland. There were scraps and pickings here, so Whisper spent less time hunting. Now she began to force the pace. Robber kept them in view but didn't approach closely so long as things went well. He noticed they were travelling now in longer stages and began to suspect that Bold would suffer.

And Bold was indeed suffering. Each day, when the time came to rest, he was exhausted. But the weather came to his rescue. The temperatures had been dropping steadily. Frost and ice formed every night. And now snow fell. A strong wind blew and they had to find shelter. Whisper led Bold to a holly bush where they found what protection they could.

**When** the blizzard ended, the two foxes were almost buried. They looked out on a wilderness of white. The snow was so thick that travelling any further just then was out of the question.

'We need to find better shelter,' Bold said, giving his coat a good shake.

'We must go underground,' Whisper agreed. 'I'll go deeper into the wood and see if I can find a burrow.'

It was a while before she came back, but she had been lucky. 'Follow me.' Bold limped after her. Under the half-exposed roots of an oak was a deserted earth. The fox pair slipped gratefully inside and slept in snatches.

When they awoke fully they found more snow had fallen. By the entrance to their shelter were a few poor fragments of food.

'Wherever did they come from?' Whisper murmured.

'It's Robber!' Bold cried joyfully. 'He hasn't forgotten us.'

Whisper knew all about Robber. 'How on earth did he find us?' she wondered.

'With his sharp black eyes,' Bold laughed.

'We need better food than this,' Whisper pointed out. 'I must go for a look around.'

'It won't be easy finding *anything*,' Bold answered crossly. 'Don't turn your nose up at such scraps. It may be all there is between us and starvation!'

## CHAPTER SEVEN

For five days the severe weather continued. Bold and Whisper remained holed up, except for the vixen's short trips for food such as bulbs or acorns which she was able to dig out of the snow. Then, on the sixth day, came milder weather and the snow began to melt.

'I think we should go on,' Whisper said. 'Your leg's well rested now.'

'All right,' Bold replied, remembering the unborn cubs, but actually feeling he would have preferred a couple more days' rest.

The ground proved to be sticky and slippery and very hard going, the worst possible conditions for Bold. He laboured on, gritting his teeth, but the slushy snow was impossible to grip and in no time his bad leg was aching, while the good ones trembled from the strain. At length he could go no further. He collapsed on to his side. Whisper came running.

'Oh Bold! What have I done to you? I shouldn't have forced you! Oh, how can I forgive myself?'

'You didn't force me,' he muttered. 'And what's

done can't be undone. I'll be better after a bit of a breather.'

Whisper knew he wouldn't. 'I'll stay with you,' she said. 'You're dangerously exposed here in the open.'

'No!' Bold insisted. 'You must take cover. No point in both of us being at risk.'

Whisper began to argue. Bold said, 'You must. For the sake of the cubs.' And the vixen crept sorrowfully away, with many a backward glance. Bold watched her heading for the nearest copse. He tried to scrape some of the snow around himself so that he stood out less in the landscape. Then exhaustion overtook him and he fell asleep.

He awoke from a troubled doze, aware he was not alone. The sun was high in the sky. He looked up – and there was Robber.

'Why are you lying here in the open?' the bird demanded. 'Where's Whisper?'

Bold explained.

'You shouldn't have tried to travel through this,' the crow said. 'Whisper should have considered you more. The thaw's well under way. A few more days would have made all the difference.'

'Don't I know it?' Bold muttered.

'I brought you this,' Robber said, nudging with his beak a lump of carrion. 'Eat it and then try to move. There's a patch of bracken not far off. You'd be better hidden there.'

'What a comfort a good friend can be,' Bold said appreciatively.

Robber cawed wisely. 'Too true.'

Bold struggled to his feet. 'I see the place you mean.' He tottered forward slowly. Robber was shocked by the poor animal's weak state. 'It'll take me a while to reach the ferns,' said Bold. 'Is there any danger?'

'No, all's clear. I'll go for more supplies.'

Somehow Bold managed to creep to the patch of vegetation. He threw himself down, panting heavily. The snow was melting fast. There were already some patches of bare ground. Robber brought more food, then retired to roost as dusk fell. With the darkness, Whisper came silently searching. She traced Bold's scent and found his makeshift shelter.

'Thank goodness you're safe,' she murmured, nuzzling him and whimpering her concern. 'From now on, we must think of you, first and foremost.'

When Bold was ready, he and Whisper continued the journey. Most of the snow had gone and food was easier to find. Whisper made no comment when Bold's pace became slower and slower still. Gradually the foxes' destination grew closer. By March they had reached the ditch where Bold had first hidden after his injury. He showed Whisper the place where he had been shot. Whisper looked solemn.

Later, with Robber always keeping a look-out for their progress, they went close to the game wood. Bold avoided it. He had no wish to see the badgers.

He was ashamed of his appearance. At last they came on to the downland.

'It won't be long now,' Bold told Whisper who was constantly asking him how much further they had to go. 'Patience has seen us through.'

'Can you keep going?' Whisper asked. 'You seem so – '

'I'll last the course,' Bold interrupted. But he knew he wouldn't. Willpower alone had kept him plodding on thus far. He would never enter White Deer Park again.

A few days later, when the Nature Reserve was almost in sight, Whisper awoke to find herself alone. She at once suspected the worst. She sought frantically for Bold in the open spaces and in the woodland. There was no sign of him. She returned to their last sleeping-quarters and waited until dusk, hoping he would appear. He didn't.

'Oh, he's gone away to die. I know it,' Whisper sobbed. 'And it's my fault: he was never up to this journey. Oh Bold!'

In the daylight again she had no choice but to go on. Her time was near and she needed safety for her cubs. She knew now that Bold had sacrificed himself for the youngsters he would never see. She found a gap in the fence and entered White Deer Park. Her first task was to find a den. A herd of white deer stepped daintily across the grass. Whisper knew her long journey was over.

That night she met another fox, a vixen like herself.

'I've never seen you around before,' said the vixen.

'No, I'm from outside the Park. I've come here so that my cubs may be born in safety,' Whisper explained.

'Indeed! And how do you know of the Reserve?'

'My cubs' father was born here.'

'Born here?' the vixen gasped. 'But . . . but . . . where is he? Oh, tell me where he is!'

Whisper said sadly, 'I can't. I don't know where he is! My brave Bold!'

'Bold!' cried the other vixen. 'I knew it! My brother cub!'

'Then you must be – '

'Charmer. Now tell me. What is your name?'

'Bold called me Whisper. Because of my stealth.'

'My brother chose well. Now, Whisper, our cubs shall be cousins. You must prepare your den while I run to my father and mother and tell them of your arrival! Then we must all hear your story.'

## CHAPTER EIGHT

Bold's last look at Whisper was one of tenderness. She lay sleeping as he left her for the last time. He was glad he had brought her close to the Park. His duty was done.

He stumbled away in the early spring sunshine. The ground was soaking wet. He entered a birch spinney which he and Whisper had passed through the previous night. Unknown to Bold, his movements were watched. Robber was following.

Bold found what he wanted – a hollow log. He bent and slunk inside. Robber waited. Bold didn't move. The crow flew over and landed by the log.

'What are you doing?' Robber asked.

'Oh!' Bold gasped. 'I thought I was alone. Robber, it's all up with me. It's only a matter of time. Whisper must finish the journey herself.'

'Don't give up, Bold,' Robber pleaded. 'Whisper will come searching for you.'

'I know. I'm going to block the entrance here with leaves and twigs. I'm done for. It's better this way.' He began to scrape some leaf litter together. Even Robber had to accept how weak and wasted Bold was. It was obvious the fox knew his end was near.

'I'll fetch you food,' Robber offered. He didn't know what else to do.

'You've been a wonderful friend,' Bold murmured. 'But, Robber, don't bother. There's no . . . point now.'

Robber flew away. He couldn't bear to watch any longer.

The next day the crow saw Whisper's hopeless search, then he followed her as she entered White Deer Park. He flew back to Bold's hideaway. The fox was still alive, but weaker than ever. Robber told him Whisper was safely home. Bold was glad. He struggled free from the log and lay on the grass in the March sunlight. 'Now I can dream,' he said.

The Farthing Wood Fox and his Vixen listened to Charmer's news with great feeling.

'I always believed Bold was still alive,' Fox said. 'We must find him and bring him home. Take us to his mate, Charmer.'

Bold's sister cub led her parents to Whisper. Friendly, Bold's brother, went with them. They greeted the young vixen as if she were already a member of their family.

'Tell us where to go,' Vixen begged. 'We can't leave Bold alone.'

'I can't give you much help,' Whisper answered sadly. 'Bold left me to . . . to . . .'

'To what?' Fox asked in agony.

'You must prepare yourselves for the worst,' Whisper said. 'Bold has suffered greatly. You must go first of all on to the downland. Head towards a patch of woodland. That's where we parted. He is under cover somewhere.'

'Will you come with us?' Charmer asked gently.

Whisper drew a shuddering breath. 'No,' she sobbed. 'I couldn't bear it.'

The foxes left the Park and, as dawn broke, they began to call to their lost relative. Robber heard them and swooped close, perching on a low branch. 'Are you the Farthing Wood Fox?' he called to the leading animal.

'Yes.'

'I can help you. Bold is my friend. I'll take you to him. Hurry, hurry!'

Bold was in no pain now. He was too weak to move but he was glad Robber had returned. He knew he wouldn't die alone. He saw the crow and he closed his eyes gratefully. When next he opened them he saw, through a mist, four familiar and beloved faces. He blinked, thinking he dreamt of being a cub again back in White Deer Park. Vixen came forward, sniffed at his poor thin body and nuzzled him tenderly.

'My brave bold cub,' she murmured.

Bold felt at peace. 'Is Whisper – ?' he began.

'Safe and well,' Vixen told him. 'We shall look after her. Your cubs will soon be born.'

Fox came close. 'They'll be fine sturdy youngsters with you for a father. My, what a fine, courageous cub you were!' He lowered his voice so that only Bold could hear his words: 'You are a brave animal.

Your adventures will be remembered as long as mine. I'm proud to be your father.'

A sigh escaped Bold's lips. He felt at peace as he realized that his life had been of value. He looked joyfully towards the black, watching figure of Robber and prepared to leave, at last, the real world.